SPACEMAN

Jane Cutler

DUTTON CHILDREN'S BOOKS

NEW YORK

My thanks to Marin Puzzle People, Inc.,
whose newsletters provided information and inspiration.

Copyright © 1997 by Jane Cutler

Library of Congress Cataloging-in-Publication Data
Cutler, Jane.
Spaceman / by Jane Cutler.
p.   cm.
Summary: Ten-year-old Gary, who is failing the fifth grade and
has trouble getting along with the other students, tries to adjust to his
learning disability and his assignment to a special education class.
ISBN 0-525-45636-8
[1. Learning disabilities—Fiction.   2. Special education—Fiction.
3. Emotional problems—Fiction.   4. Schools—Fiction.]   I. Title
PZ7.C985Sp   1997   [Fic]—dc21   96-46224   CIP   AC

Published in the United States by
Dutton Children's Books, a division of Penguin Books USA Inc.
375 Hudson Street, New York, New York 10014
Designed by Ellen M. Lucaire
Printed in USA   First Edition
4   6   8   10   9   7   5   3

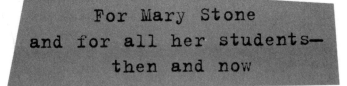

For Mary Stone
and for all her students—
then and now

SPACEMAN

Chapter One

Gary Harris thought things were as bad as they could be. But he was wrong. The year Gary went into the fifth grade, everything got worse.

Gary's fifth-grade teacher, Mr. Rudolph, was brand-new. He was young and peppy, and strict. He moved quickly. He talked fast. He used big words, and he didn't like to have to repeat what he said.

Mr. Rudolph wanted every single one of his students to be sharp all the time. "Stay with us, now, Gary," Mr. Rudolph said, when Gary looked confused. "Spunk up, Gary," Mr. Rudolph said, when Gary drooped. "For heaven's sake, be careful!" he exclaimed when Gary knocked things over or bumped into other people.

From the very first day of school, Mr. Rudolph had his eagle eye on Gary. The teacher noticed everything about him.

What Mr. Rudolph did not seem to notice was the way some of the other boys slid down in their seats and gave each other looks when the teacher spoke to Gary this way. And he didn't seem to notice when shrimpy Warren Firestone said to Gary, "Here's yours, stupid," when Warren handed back the weekly spelling tests.

One Friday afternoon near the end of September, Mr. Rudolph gave Gary a large envelope to take home. "Be sure you give this to your parents," the teacher said. "Don't lose it. And don't forget."

Gary waited for Mr. Rudolph to tell him what was in the envelope, but the teacher didn't. "Run along, Gary," he said.

Gary stuffed the envelope into his backpack and left.

Going home from school, Gary always took a long way around. The other kids who walked in his direction cut across the soccer field. But Gary tried to stay away from other kids. If they were older or younger than Gary, they'd probably leave him alone. But if he ran into boys from his class, he could usually count on trouble.

"Hey, Gary," Warren Firestone would say, pretending to stumble for no reason, the way Gary sometimes did.

"Duh, hi, Gary, uh, duh," Randy Rasmussen would call out, laughing and crossing his eyes.

Sometimes the boys would run in a circle around Gary, whooping and teasing. David Fedder would pull the hood on Gary's sweatshirt up over his head. Scotty Jones would yank it down. Warren would shove Gary toward Randy, and Randy would shove him back toward Warren. "Nah, nah, nah," the boys would yell.

Gary knew better than to cry. That would only make things worse. He knew if he ran away, they would run after him. And he also knew that if he just spaced out and stood there, they would lose interest and leave him alone.

Gary wanted to fight back, but he was afraid to try to fight so many boys at the same time. And he was afraid that if he ever did manage to get hold of one of those boys and hit him, he might never stop.

So Gary would stare into space and stand as still as he could, as still as a statue or a tree. He would pretend he was a thing that had no feelings, until the other boys got tired of teasing and ran on.

In his mind, Gary plotted ways of getting even. He would sock David Fedder in the nose. He would punch Scotty Jones in the stomach. He wasn't sure what he would do to Warren Firestone. Warren was the worst of them all. He was nearly always the one who started the trouble.

Sometimes, before his mother got home from work, Gary took the pillows off his bed and hers and punched and karate-chopped them and threw them roughly around his room. He pretended that the four pillows were his enemies and that he was fighting them all at the same time and that he was winning the fight. He punched and chopped and slammed the pillows onto the floor until they all begged for mercy. He imagined the Warren Firestone pillow crying out, "I give! I give!"

It felt good to punch pillows. But it didn't change anything.

The Friday Mr. Rudolph gave him the envelope, Gary took the longest way home. When he got to the alley between the drugstore and the grocery, he ducked in and sat down on the ground behind some empty boxes. Then he pulled the big envelope out of his backpack.

Inside, Gary found his spelling tests, a bunch of

his work sheets and other papers, and a long note from Mr. Rudolph, written in cursive. Gary had trouble reading almost everything. He couldn't read cursive at all. Still, he sat and stared at the note for a long time, trying and trying to figure out what Mr. Rudolph was saying to his parents.

Gary knew his mother would be upset if she saw his schoolwork. The papers were messy, and they all had holes in them where he'd erased and erased.

Even worse, on the top of every single test and every single paper, Mr. Rudolph had drawn a picture of a sad face and had written "F" and "*Try harder!*" with his red pen. Gary had gotten an F on everything he'd done so far in the fifth grade. And he did not know how to try any harder.

Gary sat in the alley for a long time. Then he stuffed the papers and the envelope and the note into the trash bin behind the drugstore.

After that, he went home.

Chapter Two

Most of the time, Gary lived with his mother in a small brown house that needed to be painted, inside and out.

On some weekends, Gary stayed with his father and stepmother in their bright new apartment high up in a tall building.

At his mother's, Gary had his own room and his own things. He had the run of the house. He could flop down on any of the shabby, comfortable furniture crowded into the place. He could put his feet up on the sofa without taking off his shoes. And he could cook whatever he felt like and leave a mess in the kitchen for his mother to clean up later.

Gary's father didn't approve. He claimed Gary's mother was too lazy to make Gary clean up after himself. He said Gary was a mess and that it was all his mother's fault.

"Soft" was Gary's father's opinion. "Your mother's soft, and she's making you soft."

Everything about Gary's mother was soft. Her face was round and soft. Her brown eyes looked sad and soft. Her body was plump and very soft. Even her voice was soft. Sometimes Gary didn't hear her come into a room, her footsteps were so soft.

Gary's mother worked in a nursing home full of very old people. Her softness was just right for the people who lived in the nursing home.

Gary's father and stepmother were not soft. They had loud voices, hard bodies, and strong opinions. When they looked at Gary, their blue eyes seemed to him as hard as stones. And neither one of them liked to sit still.

They each jogged seven miles a day, and they owned a gym full of hard, shiny equipment. People came to the gym to walk and run on treadmills, climb fake stairs, row boats that sat on the floor, ride stationary bicycles, ski on cable-driven machines, and lift tons of weights. They came to do everything they could to make their bodies as tough and hard as Gary's father's and stepmother's.

But nobody could outdo the two of them. Except

when they were asleep, they were in motion. No-body could call them lazy!

Gary took after his mom. Tall for his age and a bit overweight, he had a quiet voice and no muscles at all, so far as he could tell. Also, every teacher he'd ever had told him he was lazy, so he knew it must be true.

Gary loved his mother, but he wished with all his heart that he could be nothing like her. He wished he could wake up one morning and find him-self as hard as his father. Then he would show those kids, and Mr. Rudolph, and everyone.

Chapter Three

On the next Friday, Mr. Rudolph asked Gary to stay after the bell.

"I haven't heard from your parents," the teacher complained. "You gave them that envelope, didn't you?"

Gary looked at the floor. Mr. Rudolph was in his usual Friday rush. He was clearing his desk as he spoke.

"I asked them to call me," he told Gary. "I said we needed to have a meeting to figure out what to do about you. I don't understand why they haven't called me back."

"They're divorced," Gary explained.

"What does that have to do with it?" asked the teacher.

Gary looked at the floor. "I didn't know which one to give the envelope to."

"That's ridiculous, Gary," Mr. Rudolph exploded. "You just give it to one or to the other."

"Well, I didn't know."

Mr. Rudolph stopped getting ready to leave. He put his hands on his hips and frowned down at Gary. "Which one of your parents did you give it to, then?" he asked.

"I didn't give it to either of them," Gary admitted.

"Then let me have it back," demanded the teacher.

Gary began to feel confused. He knew Mr. Rudolph was about to accuse him of being lazy and careless, of not paying attention, of not doing what he was supposed to do. He wanted to run away. He wanted to put his hands over his ears and scream, the way he had once when he was a first-grader and the teacher scolded him in front of the whole class.

"I said, give me back the envelope, Gary, and I'll get in touch with your parents."

"I lost it," Gary lied.

"Lost it?" asked Mr. Rudolph.

"I lost it last week, after school. I was playing with my friends and somebody stole it out of my backpack. I mean, I left it someplace."

Mr. Rudolph sighed, to show Gary how frustrated he was. Then he let him go.

Mr. Rudolph called Gary's mother and his father. There would be a meeting at the school. They were both expected to come, and so was Gary. It was important, and it couldn't be put off.

The meeting was on Wednesday afternoon. Gary's mother left work early to get there. Gary's father and his wife, Goldy, both showed up. Mr. Rudolph was there, and Mrs. Fong, the principal, and Ms. Hernandez, the new special education teacher. They all met in Mrs. Fong's office. "I don't want to be interrupted," the principal told the school secretary. Then she closed the door.

Mr. Rudolph spoke first. "Gary is having trouble keeping up again this year," he said. "His math is below grade level, and he can barely read. He should not be in fifth grade."

Gary's father interrupted. "Of course Gary can read," he said. "I've seen him read. What are you talking about?" He glared at Mr. Rudolph.

"Gary can read on about a second-grade level.

He can't read nearly well enough to manage in fifth," said Mr. Rudolph.

To Gary's surprise, his father seemed to be angry at the teacher. "Look here," Mr. Harris argued, "are you trying to tell me that you interrupted my day and took me away from my place of business to say that my son's not reading well enough for you to teach him?

"Let me tell you something," he continued. "Reading is not the most important thing in the world. I can read just fine, and so can my wife here, and we never read a darned thing. We don't have the time. In this day and age, it's just not necessary."

His wife, Goldy, backed him up. "That's right," she said. "Nobody needs to read hardly at all anymore. Everything's on TV or on video or right there in the computer. Whatever you want. You're a teacher, Mr. Rudolph. You should know that."

There was silence in the room. Gary's father and Goldy sat back in their chairs. They looked satisfied. Gary's mother looked upset, as if she might cry. The teachers and the principal looked puzzled.

Mr. Rudolph tried again. "Gary doesn't read well enough to keep up with fifth-grade work, Mr. Harris.

He's falling farther and farther behind. I don't know how he got promoted to the fifth grade, to tell you the truth. But he did. And now we have to face some unpleasant facts: He's behind in everything, and there's nothing I can do about it. I have twenty-nine other students to teach, and your son seems to need a teacher all his own."

Gary's father glared at Mr. Rudolph. Mr. Rudolph glared back.

Mrs. Fong cleared her throat. "Mr. Harris," she said, "we believe it is still necessary for children to learn to read. But this isn't just about reading. Gary is having trouble in all areas. His academics are poor. And his social and emotional and even his physical development seem—well, delayed."

"Meaning what?" demanded Gary's father.

"Meaning he can't get along with the other kids and it makes it just about impossible for me to teach anybody anything!" Mr. Rudolph exploded.

Gary's father tilted his chair back onto two legs and squinted at Mr. Rudolph. "It seems to me you're having trouble controlling your class, young man, and that you're trying to put the blame on my son."

Mrs. Fong broke in again. "Mr. Harris, Gary's academic and social problems make it hard for everyone, Mr. Rudolph included. But most of all, this is hard for Gary."

For the first time since they started arguing, the adults seemed to remember that Gary was in the room. They all looked at him. Ms. Hernandez, who had been furiously taking notes, stopped writing. Gary's mother, who had been staring at the purse in her lap, looked up. Gary's father frowned in his direction. Goldy stared at Gary as if she'd never seen him before in her life. And Mr. Rudolph looked at him as if he might want to apologize for something.

But Gary didn't look at any of them. Gary was spacing out, staring out the window, showing them that he wasn't paying attention and that he hadn't heard a single word they'd said.

Chapter Four

After more wrangling, it was decided that Gary would be tested by Ms. Hernandez, the special education teacher. She would see if she could figure out why he was having so many problems. Gary had been tested before, when he first started having trouble in school. But Ms. Hernandez wanted to repeat some of the tests. And there were new ones she wanted to try.

Ms. Hernandez asked Gary to come to her office, just to talk, first thing the next morning.

Gary hated tests. Just thinking about taking a test made him scared and mad. So he took his time getting to the gray, trailer-like building at the rear of the school where Ms. Hernandez worked.

He knew the way well enough, because in second grade he'd spent part of every single school day there, working with Mr. Norris, a different special education teacher.

Mr. Norris had explained that Gary had learning disabilities and needed special help because there was something different about the way his brain worked. "Not your fault," Mr. Norris had said. "But something you have to live with. People don't outgrow their learning disabilities. They have to find ways to learn in spite of them."

Mr. Norris had helped Gary keep up with his reading and his math just well enough for Gary to be promoted from the second to the third grade.

Then Mr. Norris left, and the school was without a special education teacher for a whole year. That made Gary happy. No special education teacher, no special education. He was through with learning disabilities, he figured, and with special help. Now here was Ms. Hernandez, making trouble for him all over again.

"Sit down, Gary," Ms. Hernandez said, in a friendly voice. "I want to explain some things to you about the testing we're going to do next week."

"I hate tests," Gary mumbled.

"I understand," Ms. Hernandez said.

"I always flunk," Gary said.

"The tests I'm going to give you are tests you can't fail," the teacher explained. "Nobody can fail them. These tests are different."

"I always flunk," Gary insisted.

"Really, you can't," Ms. Hernandez assured him. "The tests don't even have right answers and wrong ones. They aren't made for people to pass or to fail. They're made to show me what your learning style is." Ms. Hernandez was looking at Gary, but Gary was staring out of the window, looking at nothing.

The teacher put her hand gently on Gary's chin and turned his head toward her. "Your learning style is the way you learn most easily," she explained. "Every single person has a learning style. And every teacher has a teaching style. Sometimes a student has a learning style that's different from most other people. If that's the case, a special teacher helps find ways to teach that student. That's me," she said, smiling, "a special education teacher."

"And what am I, then," Gary asked, "besides dumb?"

"What you are, I think, is a student with complicated and unusual learning styles who needs to be taught in ways that regular classroom teachers just don't have time for," Ms. Hernandez explained. "I'll know better after we have the results of the tests. Do you see?"

Gary didn't see. Why did he have to be different? Why did things have to be complicated? Why did he have to take tests? And what would happen when he flunked all of them and Ms. Hernandez found out how dumb he really was?

Gary left feeling slow and mean. He took his time going back to Mr. Rudolph's room. When he got there, the classroom was empty. Everyone had gone outside for recess.

Gary wandered out onto the playground, not paying any attention to where he walked. Suddenly he tripped over Warren Firestone, who had bent down to tie his shoe.

"Watch it, spacecase," Warren said rudely, jumping to his feet and giving Gary a shove.

Gary stumbled right into David Fedder. David pushed Gary back toward Warren. Warren shoved Gary again, harder. Randy and Scotty and Jonah were there, and they shoved him, too.

None of the boys pushed hard enough to hurt a kid as big as Gary or to knock him down, only hard enough to keep him off balance and make him look foolish. The same old game.

But this time, Gary surprised everyone, including himself.

Instead of silently staring into space while the boys teased him, Gary did something nobody expected. He stuck his arms straight out at his sides and started turning around. He turned slowly at first, then faster and faster and faster, until he was spinning in a furious circle while out of his wide-open mouth came a loud, ugly, wordless, scary noise.

Randy, David, Scotty, and Jonah scattered. But Warren smiled that sarcastic smile of his and slowly walked toward Gary.

When Warren got close, Gary stopped spinning, dropped his arms, and fell silent. Warren pointed his finger at him and laughed out loud.

That was when Gary lunged at Warren, grabbed the smaller boy around the waist, held him tightly with both arms, and lifted him off the ground.

Warren struggled. "Let go of me, you moron!" he shouted.

Gary held tight. And the more Warren hollered and struggled, the tighter Gary gripped him.

Slowly the other boys came closer. They stared at the stony Gary and the struggling Warren. Then they danced around, waving their arms and trying to get Gary's attention. They yelled, "Let go of him!" They yelled, "Put him down!"

But Gary stood as still as a post, stared off into space, and kept both arms clamped around Warren Firestone.

Finally Warren twisted so fiercely that Gary lost his hold for a split second. When he got it back, Warren had slipped. Now the angry, red-faced boy was nearly upside down, with his feet waving in the air to one side of Gary's shoulder and his head close to the ground.

"Let me go, you retard!" Warren screeched.

Now Gary heard him. And he heard the other kids, too. Suddenly, all the confusing noises of the playground rushed into his ears, along with the yells of a group of angry boys who were moving closer and closer. "Let him go! Let him go!"

Gary had no idea what he wanted to do next. So he did what everyone was telling him to do. He let go.

Warren hit the ground headfirst. He lay still for a second; then he howled and doubled up, holding his arms over his head.

Scotty rushed over to Warren, and the rest of the boys stood gaping at Gary. Nobody said anything. Out of the corner of his eye, Gary saw Mr. Rudolph hurrying toward them. "What's going on here?" the teacher demanded.

"Gary picked Warren up and threw him down on his head!" David Fedder told the teacher.

"I did not!" Gary objected, feeling frightened and cloudy. "I did not!"

"Did too!" yelled David Fedder.

"Did too!" shouted others.

"Go to Mrs. Fong's office, Gary," Mr. Rudolph ordered, "and wait there for me."

The teacher turned to Warren, who was still on the ground holding his head and whimpering. "Can you walk to the nurse's office, Warren?" Mr. Rudolph asked. He helped Warren get up and held his arm as they went. The other boys followed.

Nobody noticed that Gary didn't go to the principal's office but instead ran back to the special education trailer and around behind it, where a wild, overgrown hill sloped steeply up, where no one was allowed to go.

Crying now, Gary clambered up the hill. The sharp, dry weeds scratched his arms. "They told me to let him go," Gary sobbed. "They all said to let go."

Gary stayed up on the hillside for a long time, until he knew that everyone was gone for the day and that no one was looking for him anymore. He lay on his back in the weeds and watched the changing sky and thought about how unfair everything was.

Small, dark birds circled above him in a large flock, taking off together and flying in formation and then circling back and landing, all at the same time. Gary wondered how they'd learned to stay together that way. He thought it was amazing that not even one of those birds fell behind the others.

When it was nearly dark, Gary made his way down the hill and hurried home.

Chapter Five

Gary was suspended from school for the rest of the week. He would have to go back on Monday to "face the music," Mr. Rudolph told Mrs. Harris on the phone.

"I just don't understand any of this, Gary," she said, sniffling. "I can't believe you'd do this."

"What? Do what?" Gary demanded rudely.

"Pick on someone younger." His mother blew her nose.

Younger! "Warren Firestone isn't someone younger!" Gary cried. "Warren Firestone is in my grade! He's always been in my grade!"

Gary's mother seemed confused. "Mr. Rudolph told me you hurt a much smaller child."

"Smaller!" Gary yelled. "Smaller, not younger. Don't you know the difference?"

"Gary," his mother said softly, "I don't like it when you speak to me that way."

"Then why don't you do something about it?" he screamed.

But his mother didn't do a thing. She never did. She just sighed and shook her head and left the room.

Gary went into the kitchen to fix himself a snack. He filled a big bowl with ice cream and left the container standing on the counter. Carelessly, he crumbled Oreo cookies on top of the ice cream, and cookie crumbs fell onto the floor. Then he opened a can of chocolate syrup and got syrup all over the can opener and all over his hands. He poured the syrup on top of the cookies and ice cream. When he opened the refrigerator to get some milk, he left chocolate fingerprints on the refrigerator. When he opened the drawer to get a spoon, he left fingerprints there, too.

By the time Gary was finished in the kitchen, it was a disaster area. Ice cream was melting, milk was getting warm, cookie crumbs were scattered around, syrup was spilled, and chocolate was on every single thing he'd touched.

Later, when Gary's mother saw the mess, she

called him. He pretended not to hear her. She came to the door of his room. "Gary," she said softly, "you've made a terrible mess in the kitchen again. The ice cream is melted and the milk is spoiling and there's chocolate all over the place. Please come and help me clean it up."

"I'll do it later," Gary mumbled. He and his mother both knew he wouldn't.

Gary's mother picked up the empty ice cream bowl and the sticky spoon and took them back to the kitchen with her. Then she cleaned up Gary's mess.

Gary had been suspended from school once before, for throwing blocks at other kids, way back in kindergarten.

He couldn't remember why he threw the blocks. But he did remember the week he was suspended. He'd watched TV and played at home. His mother or a baby-sitter had stayed with him the whole time. They read him stories.

Back then, Gary had loved stories. He had a lot of books, and he would pretend to read them when nobody was around.

Gary still loved those books. Sometimes he took them to bed with him and read them out loud to himself before he went to sleep. It was the books that came later, the ones he couldn't read and that nobody read out loud to him—those were the books he hated. Those were the books he scribbled in, even though he knew he'd get in trouble for it.

Gary wondered why he was able to read the old books and not the new ones. He wondered if there were any books for older kids that he would like. Probably not, he decided. Books for kids his age wouldn't be storybooks anyway. They would be books about science and history and spelling and math.

What difference did it make? He hated books now.

Chapter Six

"Go back to your classroom for the rest of the day, Gary," Ms. Hernandez said, when all the testing was done. "I'll go over the results of these tests and decide what will be best for you. We'll know in a day or two what your new schedule will be."

Gary stared at her as if he didn't understand what she was telling him.

"I'm sure you'll be spending at least part of your day in one of the special education classes," the teacher said in a businesslike way.

Gary knew that would only make everything worse. He knew what it felt like to come back to your regular class after spending part of the day in special education. He had done it before. When you came back, you felt more left out than ever. Nobody wanted you back. And if you had any friends, by the time you turned up again, they had other friends instead.

"I don't want to do that," Gary told Ms. Hernandez.

"Don't want to do what?" she asked.

"Go back and forth."

"Gary, I want you to go to Mr. Rudolph's class. Now. Right now," said Ms. Hernandez firmly. "Tell him we're finished testing and I'll discuss the results with him after school tomorrow. Then he and Mrs. Fong and I will decide what will be best for you."

"Should I tell him I flunked them all?" Gary asked angrily.

"These are not tests you can flunk! How many times do I need to explain that to you, Gary?" Ms. Hernandez raised her voice for the first time. Gary felt better when she did. It proved to him that she was just like the others.

Gary skulked back to his classroom. He stood outside the door for a few minutes, listening to Mr. Rudolph and the students discuss a social studies project.

Gary had his jacket on. He had his lunch with him, since he'd gone straight to Ms. Hernandez when the morning bell rang. He didn't have any reason to go back to class if he didn't want to.

Unsure, he hung around for a few minutes more. Then he decided to go in. But when he opened the door and all the kids and the teacher stopped talking and looked at him, he changed his mind. He didn't go in. He stood holding the door open and yelled at them.

"I flunked all the stupid tests, you dummies!" he yelled. Then he turned and ran away as quickly as he could: down the steps and across the playground, over the soccer field, and off school grounds. He ran as if a pack of hungry wolves were chasing him.

But nobody was chasing him. Nobody came after him. Nobody called, "Wait, Gary!" Nobody cared that Gary yelled at his teacher and his whole class and then ran away. And nobody was coming to make him go back to school, where he knew he was supposed to be.

Relieved and disappointed, Gary stopped running.

Sadly, he wandered around his neighborhood, down the streets lined with small houses and, farther along, streets lined with shops.

He stopped at Dunkin' Donuts and fished seventy-five cents out of his pocket to buy an apple fritter. Then he sat down at one of the tables to eat it.

Two policemen came in and brought their coffee and doughnuts over to a table near Gary's. If they thought anything about a kid his age being out of school in the middle of the morning, they didn't show it.

The other customers sat alone, drinking coffee and eating doughnuts. Several read newspapers. One woman wrote in a notebook. A tall, raggedy man stirred a lot of sugar into his coffee and talked to himself. Where were all these people supposed to be? Gary wondered. Where did they belong?

When he finished eating his fritter, Gary looked out the big window along the side of the shop. At first, he watched the people walking by, the cars passing, the streetcars coming and going. But after a while, he stopped seeing these things. After a while, he emptied his mind and just sat, feeling nothing, staring into space.

Chapter Seven

On the following Monday morning, Mr. Rudolph wrote the week's spelling words on the board and told the class to copy them. Then he asked Gary to come up to his desk.

"What about my spelling words?" Gary asked.

Everyone looked up from their work.

"Just come here, Gary," the teacher repeated impatiently.

Gary put his pencil down on his desk, but it rolled to the edge and fell off. He bent over to pick it up, and his paper slid onto the floor. The other kids laughed.

"Boys and girls, settle down," Mr. Rudolph warned.

Gary picked up the pencil and the paper and set them on his chair. Then he went up to the teacher's desk.

Mr. Rudolph spoke firmly to Gary. "Get your jacket and your backpack and your lunch," the teacher said, "and anything in your desk that belongs to you. Then report to Ms. Hernandez."

Gary's chin was on his chest. "What about my spelling words?" he asked.

"You don't need to worry about them," Mr. Rudolph said. "You're going to be in special education full-time now, remember?"

Of course Gary remembered. Ms. Hernandez had told him on Friday. But he was stalling. He didn't want to leave the fifth grade. He didn't even want to leave Mr. Rudolph. He didn't want to go to a full-time special ed class.

"Get your things, Gary," Mr. Rudolph repeated.

"I don't want to go," said Gary in a tiny voice.

"What?" demanded the teacher. "Speak up, Gary."

"Please can I have another chance?" Gary begged.

Mr. Rudolph put his hand right in the middle of Gary's back and guided him into the coatroom. He watched while Gary got his things.

"Is there anything personal in your desk?" the teacher asked. Gary shook his head no. There might be. He couldn't remember what was underneath the mess inside his desk. And he didn't want to look. "All right, then," said Mr. Rudolph, walking with Gary to the door of the fifth-grade classroom.

The two of them stepped outside. Gary heard the other students start to giggle. Mr. Rudolph heard them, too. He closed the door. "Good-bye, Gary," he said stiffly. "Stop by someday and let me know how you're doing."

Then the teacher turned and went back inside, leaving Gary by himself.

All the classroom doors were closed. It was 9:15 Monday morning. Every single class in the whole school, Gary knew, was copying the week's new spelling words off the board. It was what they always did first thing on Monday morning.

It turned out that Gary wouldn't be in Ms. Hernandez's class, either. "Because of the serious trouble you're having getting along with other children," Ms. Hernandez told Gary, "you've been assigned to the county Special Needs class.

"Starting tomorrow, a minibus will pick you up at your house and take you home after school, too.

But today you can walk. Just follow the path on up the hill to the next building. When you get there, give this folder to the teacher. Her name is Mrs. Block, and she's expecting you."

"I thought I was supposed to be in your class!" Gary cried.

"That was before you started dropping people on their heads, Gary," Ms. Hernandez told him.

"One person!" Gary protested.

Ms. Hernandez shook her head. "I'm sorry, Gary," she said. "But it turns out special education students with serious behavior problems have to go to the county class. Mrs. Fong checked with the district office. That's the rule now."

Gary had never even heard of another special education class. He couldn't have been more shocked if they had told him to go to school on the moon.

Ms. Hernandez pushed a fat folder into Gary's hands. "These are your test results and reports from the school psychologist and all your teachers. You're making a fresh start today, so I'm trusting you to give the folder to Mrs. Block. I'm sure you won't disappoint me."

Ms. Hernandez went outside with Gary and gave

him a gentle push forward. Then she disappeared back into her office.

Gary stood by himself for a minute holding the folder in his hands. His jacket was scrunched under one arm and his backpack with his lunch inside it hung over his shoulder.

Then, slowly, he began to trudge up the path. He felt afraid. He wondered how long a walk it would be to get to this class he'd never heard about before. He wondered what kind of wild kids might be there. Behavior problems! Kids who would steal your stuff. Kids who would beat you up. Kids who would come to school with knives, maybe guns. Bad kids.

Gary wanted more than anything to go home. But when he thought about how his mother would cry and his father would yell, he knew he couldn't. There was nothing he could do now but go to this special class, where he imagined a bunch of weirdos sitting around making rude remarks, maybe even threats, while the teacher tried to get them to do their Monday morning spelling.

The gray shadow of the trailer where Ms. Hernandez worked was out of sight behind him. Still the narrow path wound on ahead. Even though the misty morning was cool, Gary started to sweat.

Maybe he would sit down and drink the apple juice out of his lunch before he went on. He was thirsty, and he wasn't in a hurry. If they were going to call him a behavior problem, he might as well be one, he thought, hating everyone.

Just then, a large red rubber ball came bouncing down the path, and behind it ran a short, chunky boy with no shoes on. "Ball up!" the boy called when he saw Gary.

Surprised, Gary let go of his stuff and grabbed for the ball. His jacket fell to the ground. So did his lunch. And so did the folder. The rubber band Ms. Hernandez had put around it broke, and all the papers spilled out.

The ball was a big one, the kind kindergartners play with, and Gary caught it easily.

"Good catch," said the boy, walking gingerly along the trail in his socks.

Gary handed over the ball and started to pick up his things. He shoved the papers back into the folder any which way while the boy stood with his arms wrapped around the ball, waiting.

"What happened to your shoes?" Gary wanted to know.

"I can't wear them at school," the boy answered.

"You can't?"

"Nope."

The boy turned and walked carefully back along the path. Gary followed him.

"Why can't you?" Gary asked.

"If I don't have my shoes, then I don't run away," the boy answered. "So I take them off and give them to Mrs. Block when I get to school in the morning. And I get them back when I go home."

"Do you run away then?" Gary wondered.

"Sometimes," the boy replied.

At the end of the path was an open, grassy playing field. Beyond it, Gary could see a one-story building that looked more like a small house than a school.

On the field stood three kids. One, a girl wearing big basketball shoes and a turned-around cap, was clumsily swinging a bat. The other two were out in the field, waiting. One boy was enormously fat. He had on baggy warm-up pants and a red shirt. The other boy was tall and skinny with short hair that stuck up on top.

"Who is that, Jesse?" the skinny boy called when he saw Gary. "Who is that behind you?" He sounded worried.

The three kids on the field stared at Gary. Gary stared back. "What're you guys playing?" he asked Jesse.

"Moonball," was the answer.

Moonball! Maybe they *were* sending him to school on the moon! "Ever played moonball?" Jesse asked. Gary shook his head. "It's like baseball," Jesse said. "Except you use this big ball. It's a lot easier to hit and catch, which is good, because most of us aren't very coordinated. Besides, when it goes into the trees, it's easy to find."

Gary remembered what Ms. Hernandez had told him to do. "Where's the teacher?" he asked.

"Hold on a minute," Jesse called to the others, "I have to take the new kid inside." He turned to Gary. "Come with me," he said.

Gary followed Jesse across the field, and the other three children followed Gary. He felt like part of a freaky parade.

When they got to the school building, Jesse pulled open the classroom door. "Hey, Mrs. Block," he called importantly, "someone new!"

Gary stepped into the room just in time to see a stern-looking woman with wild red hair and pale, freckled skin rise up from behind the tall stacks of papers and textbooks and workbooks, which were littered all over a rickety-looking table.

"Hey?" the woman inquired, frowning. "Hay is for horses, I believe."

Jesse clamped down on a giggle. "Sorry, Mrs. Block."

"Go out and start over," the woman said, sitting down and disappearing behind the clutter.

Gary wondered if he should go up to the teacher's table or wait by the door.

"Come on," Jesse tugged his arm.

"Come on where?" Gary wanted to know.

"Outside," Jesse answered. "We have to do it over."

"Do what over?" asked Gary.

"Come in over. I did it wrong. I said the wrong thing, so we have to do it over."

"I didn't say the wrong thing," Gary told him. "I didn't say anything. Why do I have to do it over?"

Jesse whispered, "Don't argue, just come on," and he tried to pull Gary out the door.

Gary pulled away. He was tired of being told to go here and go there.

Just then, the pale, frowning teacher rose up from behind the jumble and clutter on her table, like a sea serpent rising out of the waves, and eyeballed the two boys scuffling in the doorway. Jesse jumped back outside. So did Gary.

"I have to do it over," Jesse explained to the others, who were still waiting.

"Shee, Jesse," the fat boy said.

"Just do it then," the skinny boy urged.

"Hurry up," said the girl, "so we can find out who he is."

Gary didn't say anything. He clutched the bulging folder, creased and dirty now. He held on to his backpack and his jacket. He felt as if he'd been carrying these things around with him all his life.

Jesse handed the ball to the girl. He tucked his shirt in, and he pulled up one dusty sock and then the other. He cleared his throat. "Follow me," he said to Gary. Then he marched to the teacher's table. Gary and the others marched right behind him.

Jesse waited for the teacher to look up from the

papers she was grading. It seemed to Gary she took her time noticing that there were five kids standing practically at her elbow. But he waited quietly, too, keeping his eye on the woman's wild, curly hair, which quivered as she worked.

Finally, she lifted her head, took off her glasses, and looked at them. "Well?" she said.

"Excuse me, Mrs. Block," Jesse said politely.

"You're excused," said the teacher. She put her glasses back on and started to work again.

The fat boy snorted.

Jesse squirmed.

Gary stared. He could feel movement behind him, and he sensed that other students were gathering there. He could hear them leaving their tables and desks and forming a curious group in back of him. But he didn't turn around. He was afraid to.

Jesse took a deep breath and tried again.

"Mrs. Block, here's a new kid."

"Kid?" Mrs. Block answered, not even looking up this time. "A baby goat? No, thank you. Not today. I put up with a lot in this class, but not with barnyard creatures."

"A new student," said Jesse, beginning to sound a little desperate.

"Pupil," someone else tried.

"Victim!" the fat boy said. All the kids laughed.

The teacher looked sharply up. "Everybody back to work!" she commanded.

Everyone scattered, except Gary.

The teacher leaned back in her chair, regarded Gary, and reached out for his mussed-up folder. "Sit down," she said, pointing to a straight-backed old chair next to her table. Gary started to sit on the chair, but workbooks were stacked on the seat, so he stood next to it.

The wild red head was bent over the papers from Gary's folder. Speedily, the teacher read them. Then she stuck them back into the folder and shoved the folder into the overflowing bottom drawer of an old wooden desk standing next to her table. Then she turned to Gary.

When she saw that Gary was still standing, she took the stack of workbooks off the chair and set them onto the floor. "Sit down," she said again. Gary sat.

"You're Gary Harris," the teacher told him. "You're ten years old, and you have special learning styles that hinder your progress in the regular classroom setting. Look at me when I speak to you, Gary.

"I'm Mrs. Block," she continued. "I have special teaching skills that can help people with special learning styles make progress in an irregular classroom setting. Or for that matter, in any setting.

"As long as . . ." Mrs. Block looked right into Gary's eyes. "As long as . . ." Mrs. Block repeated, hooking his eyes with hers and holding them fast.

"As long as there is no dropping of anyone on his or her head. Because if there is anything of the sort," Mrs. Block continued, "anything of the sort," she emphasized, "the consequences will be dire."

Gary stared, eyes wide.

"What does *dire* mean?" Mrs. Block asked.

"I don't know," Gary said. His voice was only a whisper.

The teacher didn't say anything. "Am I supposed to look it up?" Gary asked.

"Only if you want to know what it means," replied the teacher.

Then she called all the other students up to her table. It was time for introductions.

Chapter Eight

Every student in Mrs. Block's class had made up an introduction, then practiced and memorized it. Now they stood in a group facing Gary and Mrs. Block, who sat behind her table and looked ready to be displeased.

"Jesse," she said, "why don't you go first?"

Jesse stepped forward, as he had been taught to do. "My name is Jesse Green," he said. "I'm eight years old. I live with my grandparents, who are too old to be bothered with a child. I'm in Mrs. Block's class because I have trouble reading. And because I run away. Mrs. Block takes charge of my shoes when I come in the morning. I know where she puts them. But I don't ever feel like running away from here. So I don't. I like the class because nobody is allowed to make fun of me, and because I'm starting to learn better."

The next student to step forward was the tall girl from the moonball game. "My name is Amanda Elizabeth Rudman," she said. "I'm twelve years old. I live with my mother and father in a big house with a swimming pool and an electric alarm system. I am in Mrs. Block's special education class because I have trouble—" Amanda stopped. She looked mixed up. Then she looked as if she might cry.

"That's good, Amanda," said Mrs. Block. "Go on. You have trouble doing what?"

"Trouble!" said Amanda. "I have trouble!"

"Okay," Mrs. Block said. "Calm down now, and tell Gary about your project."

Amanda took a deep, shaky breath. Then she nodded toward one corner of the room. Gary saw a kind of pen with a tawny puppy curled up asleep inside. "I'm raising a puppy to be a guide dog for the blind," she said. "And—" Amanda was stuck again. She looked panicky.

"Do you like this class?" Mrs. Block asked.

"Yes," said Amanda.

"Can you tell Gary why?" the teacher coached.

Amanda took a deep breath and then spoke so quickly that Gary could hardly understand her. "I like the class because even though I don't get along well with people, Mrs. Block doesn't let me get into fights. The end."

"Who wants to go next?" the teacher asked.

The fat boy stepped forward. "My name is Richard Robertson," he said. "I'm eleven years old and way bigger than anyone else my age. It's hard for me to get along with other kids because they make fun of me, and then I get mad and sit on them. Also, I'm dyslexic, which means I have trouble with reading. I procrastinate and daydream. I never finish what I start. I'm disorganized. And I'm not too good with numbers, neither."

"Either," Mrs. Block corrected.

"Either," he said. "My dad's a lawyer, and my mother is a computer programmer, and they're worried about what will become of me. I just started in Mrs. Block's class a couple of weeks ago, and so far I like it. Except that Mrs. Block hasn't figured out yet how to teach me."

A small boy with bright brown eyes stepped forward. "My name is Alec Chen," he said briskly. "And I'm in Mrs. Block's special education class because I'm—incorrigible."

Some of the kids giggled. Gary wondered what

incorrigible meant. Mrs. Block snorted. "Smart alec," she said.

One by one, other students introduced themselves. Most of them said they couldn't read or write very well. Some said they couldn't follow directions or concentrate. Every single one of them had trouble learning things. One boy spoke so unclearly that Gary could not understand him at all. The boy said something and then pointed to his throat. He said something else and held up his hands.

"I can't understand him," Gary told the teacher.

The boy looked disappointed.

"Marshall is telling you that he has a disease called cerebral palsy," Mrs. Block told Gary.

"He has it in his throat and in his hands," Richard added.

"You'll understand Marshall better after you've been around him for a while," said Mrs. Block. "And if you can't understand, he will type out what he's trying to say on the computer."

"And if you can't read it, he'll get mad!" said Alec.

The students, including Marshall, all laughed.

One girl, Katherine, said that she was hyperactive and had trouble with self-control. She said that when she began to feel as if she might explode, she asked Mrs. Block for permission to run around the building until she felt better. "Like right now!" she cried.

"Get going," said the teacher. And off Katherine went, round and round the building, running by the windows and waving to the others as she passed.

A few children refused to introduce themselves. Mrs. Block didn't force them.

"Now, Gary, how about you? Why don't you introduce yourself to the others?" the teacher suggested.

"What should I say?" Gary asked. He looked at the students. Every eye was on him. "Tell us your name," prompted Mrs. Block.

"Gary Harris," Gary said. Then he stopped and looked back at the teacher.

"Tell them how old you are, what grade you're in, and why you're in this class," she instructed.

Gary started over, feeling shy. "My name is Gary Harris," he repeated softly.

"I can't hear him," someone complained.

Gary took a deep breath and began again, talking

loudly and quickly, to get the introduction over with.

"My name is Gary Harris. I'm ten. I get mixed up and space out a lot. I just got kicked out of the fifth grade. Everyone is mad at me because I . . . because I accidentally hurt someone. I have trouble learning everything," he concluded, "and no friends."

Gary took a deep breath and looked defiantly at the other children.

"Time for lunch," said Mrs. Block.

Chapter Nine

The lunchroom, next door to the main classroom, had a lot of cupboards, a sink and a refrigerator, several tables, dishes and cups and silverware. It had everything a kitchen in a home would have. The children got out their lunches and drinks and sat down to eat. There was a lot of poking and pushing, laughing and noise. Gary began to feel grumpy and confused. He got his lunch and sat down with the crumpled brown bag in front of him, but he didn't open it.

Before long, someone's drink was spilled and someone else's sandwich was grabbed, and a fight almost started but didn't. Then Katherine, who had been running around and around the building all this time, burst in. "Water!" she gasped. Jesse got her some. After she drank it, she sank onto a bench and put her head down in her arms on the table next to it. She was sweating. Her wet shirt stuck to her back. She closed her eyes. "I'm too tired to eat," she said.

"Why don't you try some of this?" Alec teased. "This'll be hard to resist." He shoved his half-eaten apple under her nose.

She opened her eyes and shoved it back. "Buzz off!" she said.

Alec jumped up onto the table. "Buzzzzz, buzzzzz, buzzz!" He hopped in a circle and waved his arms.

Mrs. Block appeared at the door to the lunchroom. She had a workbook in one hand and a marking pen in the other. She frowned at Alec, who ignored her. "Buzzzz! Buzzzz!"

Katherine grabbed for his ankle, but he jumped away. "Buzzzzzz!"

"No dancing on the tables without written permission from your parents, Alec," Mrs. Block said. She vanished without another word. Gary wondered what in the world she was talking about.

"Get down, Alec," Jesse complained. "It's my week to clean up, and I'll never get the germs cleaned off the table from your shoes."

"Get down," Katherine repeated, irritably grabbing at Alec's leg.

"In-corri-gi-ble!" sang Alec, leaping off the table as if off a trampoline. "Alec, the Olympic athlete, wins the table-dancing competition!" Now he strutted around the lunchroom. "A gold medal for Alec Chen, representing Mrs. Block's Blockheads, from the USA!" he announced.

"Who wants to play Capture the Flag?" Amanda asked. Everyone stuffed the rest of their lunches into the garbage can and made for the door. Jesse got out the broom and the dustpan and the soap and the sponge and started to clean up.

"Aren't you going to eat?" he asked when he saw Gary still sitting at the table, looking at nothing.

Gary didn't answer.

Jesse came over and stood right by him. "I said, aren't you going to eat?" he repeated loudly.

"Oh," said Gary, "no."

"You'll be hungry later," Jesse warned.

"Probably," Gary admitted.

"Don't worry about it," Jesse said. "Mrs. Block will let you eat whenever you're hungry."

"She will?" Gary was surprised to hear this.

Jesse swept the crumbs out from under the table. "Mrs. Block doesn't think people can learn much when they're hungry," he explained.

Gary opened his lunch bag and took out the peanut butter and jelly sandwich his mother had made for him and the container of apple juice and the chocolate-chip cookies. He ate slowly, staring off into space and not trying to make sense out of anything.

After the lunch recess was over, some of the students knew what they were supposed to do next. Others gathered around Mrs. Block's table for instructions.

Computers were turned on. Two aides, Mr. Cato and Ms. Sullivan, arrived. Soon all the classrooms hummed with the special sound of people busy working. Everyone except Gary seemed to have something to do. He stood a few feet away from the teacher's table and waited, feeling angry and left out.

Finally he asked crossly, "Mrs. Block, what am I supposed to do this afternoon?"

"Ooops!" she said. "Sorry, Gary!" Then she tapped her front teeth with the eraser end of her pencil and thought.

"This afternoon," Mrs. Block said finally, "I want you to watch the baby."

"What baby?" asked Gary.

"Ms. Sullivan's baby," Mrs. Block answered. "He's sleeping in his playpen in the kitchen. His baby-sitter is sick and couldn't come to their house to take care of him, so Ms. Sullivan brought him to school with her. I want you to watch him."

"Watch him sleep?"

"Watch him sleep and wake up and whatever else he does. Watch everything he does until—can you tell time, Gary?" Gary nodded. "Until two o'clock. That's one hour from now. Then report back to me.

"I want you to think of two or three words to describe what you observe about the baby between now and two o'clock."

"Two or three words?"

"No more than that," the teacher cautioned. "One word might even be enough, if you can come up with exactly the right one."

Gary went back into the lunchroom. Ms. Sullivan had left the playpen with the baby in it out in the middle of the floor. The baby was lying on its stomach. It had on overalls and a T-shirt. It had on one shoe. It had hair that stuck up all around its head.

Gary wondered if the baby was a girl or a boy.

57

He went and stood in the doorway between the two rooms until Mrs. Block noticed him. "I thought you were watching the baby," she said.

"I am," Gary said. "I mean, I was."

"Why did you stop?" she asked.

"I wanted to know the baby's name."

"Why?"

"So I can talk to it when it gets up. So I know if it's a boy or a girl."

Mrs. Block looked at him steadily. Gary looked down. "I guess I shouldn't have interrupted," he said.

"Of course you should interrupt when you need to," the teacher contradicted. "And you should look at people when you talk to them.

"The baby's name is Patrick Donovan Marcus Sullivan," she told him. "How's that for a moniker?"

"Moniker?" asked Gary.

"Name," she explained. "We call him Pat."

Gary nodded and went back to watch the baby, who was still fast asleep.

After about ten minutes, he heard laughter coming from the other room and went to the doorway to see what everyone else was doing that was so much fun. Mrs. Block saw him standing there and raised her eyebrows at him.

"I'm tired of watching the baby," Gary said. "Don't we take turns baby-sitting?"

"Baby-sitting!" exclaimed Mrs. Block. "You are not baby-sitting! You are investigating. You are conducting an experiment. You are observing and, on the basis of your observation, you are going to draw a conclusion. You're about to have a learning experience. Better get back in there before you miss it!"

Gary could see that Amanda was taking her puppy outside on its red leash. He would much rather have observed the puppy learn how to be a guide dog for the blind than watch a baby sleep.

But Pat didn't sleep the whole time. He woke up and rubbed his nose and his eyes with his fists. Then he started to cry, but he stopped when he saw Gary.

Next, Pat picked up a small stuffed dog and threw it out of the playpen onto the floor. He picked up a soft square block and threw that out, too. He picked up all the toys in his playpen and threw them out. Then he looked at Gary and waited.

Gary waited, too.

Pat's face scrunched up. He pointed at his toys. He whimpered.

Gary picked up the toys and put them back into

the playpen. The baby threw them all out again. He looked at Gary and waited.

Gary waited, too.

Pat's face scrunched up again. He pointed. He started to cry.

"Okay, okay," Gary said, putting the toys back again.

Pat smiled at Gary. He played with his toys for a few seconds. Then over the top of the playpen sailed the stuffed dog and the soft block. Over the top of the playpen came one toy after another.

Pat waited.

Gary waited.

"No," Gary said, feeling stubborn. Pat pointed. He whimpered. Gary shook his head. "No," he said.

Pat howled.

Gary looked toward the classroom, hoping help was on its way.

Mrs. Block stuck her head into the lunchroom. "I think he wants to get out," Gary said quickly.

"Maybe," she responded. "Can you think of anything else he might want?"

"Maybe he wants to eat?"

"His mom says he ate just before his nap." The

teacher paused. "Maybe he wants you to pick up his toys for him."

"I already did," Gary told her. "Twice."

"Maybe he wants you to do it again."

"I don't want to do it again," Gary said. "Why does he keep throwing his toys out if he wants them in?" he asked.

"Why do you think?"

"I don't know."

"Well, think about it. Think about what he's doing and about what he wants you to do. Think of a word or two or three that would describe the way Pat is acting." The teacher disappeared. Gary tried to think. The baby pointed and wailed.

Finally Gary stormed to the doorway. "Mrs. Block," he fumed, "this baby will not stop crying. If I give him his toys, he throws them out. After he throws them out, he wants them back."

"You sound frustrated," Mrs. Block said calmly.

"I am frustrated."

"And you sound angry."

"I am angry."

"You sound as if you want Pat to learn something the first time you try to teach it to him. You sound as if you want Pat to learn something he may not be ready to learn.

"Will someone please remind Gary what sort of class this is?" Mrs. Block asked.

"A special education class," Loretta called out.

"Where people have individual learning styles," Richard added.

"Where teachers have to figure out special ways to teach so the special students can learn," sang Alec.

"I guess you haven't figured out how to teach Pat in a way he's ready to learn. Or maybe you've misunderstood what Pat has in mind. Maybe he's not trying to annoy you."

"He might be trying to make friends," Jesse suggested.

"He might," agreed the teacher.

Gary did not feel encouraged. "Anyway, it's almost two o'clock," he said as he went back into the lunchroom.

But Ms. Sullivan, who didn't know about Gary's assignment, bustled in right behind him. "That'll be enough of that, young man!" she said to Pat, scooping up the fussy baby and taking him back with her into one of the smaller classrooms, where she and a small group of children were working.

Once again, Gary was the only one who wasn't busy. He thought about sneaking outside to watch Amanda and the puppy. He wondered how much trouble he'd be in if he got caught. Just then, Mrs. Block came into the lunchroom and went over to the sink to wash her hands.

"Ready to give me your report?" she asked.

"Report?"

"Yes, your report about the baby. Now that you've finished observing him, what words have you thought of that best describe him?"

"Don't I have to write it, if it's a report?" asked Gary, stalling.

"This is an oral report. You just have to tell me."

Gary thought. "The baby is—dumb."

"Dumb," said the teacher.

"Stupid," Gary tried.

"Stupid," repeated the teacher.

"Uncooperative," Gary said, remembering the things teachers had said about him. "Lazy."

Mrs. Block waited. Gary could tell she wasn't satisfied with any of the words. "And crabby," he concluded.

The teacher dried her hands. "Harsh words to use to describe someone," she said, tossing the paper towel toward the wastebasket and hitting the floor next to it.

"It's not my fault," Gary said.

"What's not?" asked Mrs. Block.

"It's not my fault if he's so babyish."

"Babyish!" said Mrs. Block. "Eureka! That's just exactly the right word for Pat. *Babyish.*

"Well done, Gary. You get an A-plus on your first assignment. I'm going to go write it down in my grade book so I don't forget."

A-plus! Gary had never gotten an A-plus on anything before in his life!

"Now your next assignment will be a real challenge," the teacher said. "I'm assigning you to help Amanda train that puppy. Lord knows she can use some help!" The teacher rolled her eyes skyward.

"You mean I get to help train the puppy as part of my schoolwork?" Gary exclaimed.

"All hands on deck here," Mrs. Block said, suddenly stern and frowning. "Lots to be done. Everyone has to pitch in. I can't do it all myself, you know."

Gary felt bold. "What about the computer?" he asked. "Do I get to work on the computer, too?"

"You must work on the computer," the teacher

declared. "You have to do everything. I have to do everything and you have to do everything. This is just like an old-fashioned one-room schoolhouse. We have a bunch of kids, no two alike, and only one teacher to run the whole show. We're like pioneers in the olden days. Everybody in this class does everything. All we need to be like a real old-timey school is a wood-burning stove and a switch."

"A switch?"

"A long willow branch or something like that. Something for the teacher to smack the pupils with. Like in the good old days." Mrs. Block thought for moment. "Actually, I think sometimes they used to hit the kids with a ruler. I've got a ruler around here somewhere."

Gary was lost. He had no idea what Mrs. Block was talking about. But he didn't feel confused the way he felt when he couldn't understand other people. He had the clear feeling that sometimes not understanding what Mrs. Block was talking about had nothing to do with him. He had the feeling that when she talked in riddles, it was her way of being friendly. Besides, he could tell she didn't intend to hit anyone with anything.

"Whew," the teacher said. "Look at the clock!"

She went back into the main classroom. "Time to clean up," she called.

Gary heard chairs scraping—and falling—and feet shuffling and voices raising as the students began to shove the furniture back to where it was when they started, to put away their materials, and to get their stuff together.

Two big boys whose names Gary couldn't remember burst into the lunchroom and tore around the tables, throwing crumpled pieces of paper at one another and laughing.

Jesse slid in. "See you tomorrow, Gary," he said, taking a pair of red high-tops out of the bat-and-ball cupboard. "Unless I run away."

"Hold on!" Gary said.

"Hold on to what?" asked Jesse.

"I mean, don't. Okay?"

"Don't run away?"

"Yeah," said Gary. "So you'll be here tomorrow."

Jesse thought. "Can't promise," he said.

"So what?" said Gary. He looked away. "Who cares?"

"Some people do," Jesse said.

"Well, not me," said Gary.

"So what?" said Jesse. "Who cares?"

Mrs. Block made the students line up at the door and quiet down before they left. She had to speak to the two bigger boys several times. The minibus was waiting in the parking lot at the very top of the hill.

"You're to walk home today, Gary," Mrs. Block told him before she went with the others to the bus. "But from now on, even though you live close by, the bus driver will be authorized to pick you up and drop you off, too."

Everyone else went on up the hill. Gary put on his jacket and his backpack and went down.

Slowly, Gary walked along the path. He felt as if a year had gone by since he came up it.

He passed Ms. Hernandez's trailer and then the other school buildings, praying he wouldn't run into anyone. But the rest of the classes weren't out yet, and there were no other kids around.

As he walked home, Gary thought about what a strange day it had been. Then he wondered why Amanda was having such a hard time training her puppy. Could dogs have learning differences? Gary hoped not. He was pretty sure it was hard enough to train a dog without having to think about special needs.

As he turned onto his block, Gary found himself hoping that Jesse would be at school in the morning. He wondered where Jesse went when he ran away. He wondered how they found him and got him to come back. He wondered why someone like Jesse would want to run away in the first place.

Before he knew it, Gary was at his own front door. Gary had started the day with nothing on his mind except how angry he was at everyone. Now he had a lot of other things to think about, and he was in a much better mood.

It didn't last.

The next morning, one of the big boys tripped Gary on purpose when Gary got on the bus. Jesse had run off and wasn't at school. And when Mrs. Block told Amanda that Gary would be helping her to train the dog, Amanda had a fit.

Before the first fifteen minutes of school were over that Tuesday morning, Gary was angry at everyone all over again.

Chapter Eleven

Jesse needed to have his shoes on to run away. But Gary didn't need anything. He could get away anytime he wanted to. He could simply space out and disappear. Or he could make everything around him disappear. It was all the same.

Sitting at his desk, standing in the middle of the room, riding on the minibus—anyplace—if Gary felt angry or mixed up enough, he would move into a place of his own where nobody else could go. He would let his eyes stare but not see. He would let his jaw drop. His face would be blank. His mind would be vacant. He would stay perfectly still and let everything around him fall away.

It was an old trick, the one that earned him the nicknames space case, space cadet, spaceout, spacy. It was the trick that gave Gary control over things that frightened him and situations he couldn't manage or understand.

Gary had plenty of reasons to space out during his first days in Mrs. Block's class. He sometimes became confused by his new surroundings. He mixed up the door to the supply closet with the door to the bathroom and got both of those doors confused with the one that opened to the outside. He got his desk mixed up with someone else's—twice—and he never, not for even one minute, felt sure about where he was or what he was doing.

If he'd been able to stop spacing out, Gary would have noticed that things in Mrs. Block's class were different from any class he'd been in before. Even though he was mixed up, even though he froze and got spacy, the people around him were patient. They all acted as if anyone could forget where his desk was or go to the wrong door over and over again.

"Gary, you're a real spaceman," Ms. Sullivan said cheerfully one afternoon, when Gary looked in the wrong desk for his English workbook.

Gary's face turned bright red. He felt angry and embarrassed.

To his surprise, the aide looked upset. "I

shouldn't have said that," she apologized. "I didn't mean to hurt your feelings. I'm very sorry."

Alec was listening. "What's wrong with being a spaceman?" he asked. "I want to be a spaceman. I want to hit a golf ball on the moon and ride in a rocket ship and be weightless and explore other planets and be famous. BLAST OFF!" he cried.

"That's an astronaut, Alec," Richard said.

"And another word for astronaut is *spaceman*—I betcha," countered Alec.

Ms. Sullivan broke in. "You kids are great," she said. "You've come up with something that might help me out. What do you think, Gary? Do you know what an astronaut is?" Gary didn't answer. "Gary?" He nodded yes. "Can you tell me?" Ms. Sullivan persisted.

"Somebody who goes up in a spaceship," Gary mumbled.

"To do what?"

"To find out things."

"Is it easy to be an astronaut?" Ms. Sullivan asked.

"Naw, it's really, really hard!" Alec broke in. "You have to be smart and strong and brave. Like ME!"

"Smart and strong and brave," Ms. Sullivan said. "That describes an astronaut perfectly."

"But what about a spaceman?" Richard asked.

"Well," she said, "an astronaut is a space explorer, and another word for a space explorer could be a spaceman. And if Gary could think of himself as smart and strong and brave, even when he feels spacy, it might help."

"What about spacegirl?" Amanda wanted to know.

"Spaceperson?" Loretta suggested.

"I get your point, ladies," Ms. Sullivan said, laughing, "but in this case, we're talking about Gary, so *spaceman* is okay."

Gary was pretending not to listen to what they were saying. But he was listening. He heard them. And he didn't mind what he heard. He even imagined himself dressed in a space suit and a helmet; floating around inside a rocket; knowing exactly what he was supposed to do every minute; and being able to do it, the way astronauts did. Smart and strong and brave, the way astronauts were.

"What do you think, Gary?" Ms. Sullivan asked.

"I think a spaceman could be the same as an

astronaut," he said. "And I think I don't mind you calling me spaceman, if that's what you meant."

"Well," she admitted, "it isn't what I meant. But it is what I mean now."

"Earth to Gary," Mr. Cato, another aide, said in a friendly way the next afternoon.

"Gary's on his way to Mars, Mr. Cato," Loretta told him. "Gary's a spaceman."

If Gary had kept track of Blame and Praise at school, he would have had two unequal lists. In the Blame column, there wouldn't have been one mark. Not one of the teachers criticized him all week long. But in the Praise column, there would have been a lot of marks. Almost everything he did, no matter how small it was, was noticed and praised by one of them. "That's right," they'd say. "Now you're getting it." Or "That's better than last time." Or "You seem to be finding your way around now."

But Gary wasn't keeping track of Blame or Praise. What Gary was keeping track of was how often he caught Mrs. Block looking at him. "She watches me every single minute," he complained to his mother.

"How can that be possible?" his mother reasoned. "She's got a whole classroom full of students. How could she spend all her time watching just one of them?"

"How should I know?" Gary grumbled.

"Maybe you're imagining it," his mother suggested.

"I am not imagining it! She watches me!" Gary replied hotly.

"Calm down, Gary," his mother said, surprising Gary with the firm tone of her voice. "I'm sure if Mrs. Block is watching you, she's doing it for a reason. She's a teacher who has spent her whole life teaching children with special needs. She's not like that Mr. Rudolph. She knows exactly what she's doing. She's someone we can trust. So I think it's time you stopped complaining."

He would stop complaining, Gary thought angrily. He would never tell his mother another thing, ever again. He would show her.

Gary spent almost the whole weekend sitting in front of the TV, spacing out, not thinking about anything and not really watching the programs, either. One time, he heard his mother talking on the telephone. "You can lead a horse to water," she was saying in that new, no-nonsense voice, "but you can't make him drink." Gary knew she was talking to his father and that they were talking about him. Ganging up on him!

Let them talk, he thought. Nobody can make me drink—or think—or anything.

Chapter Twelve

But when the following Monday came, Mrs. Block was ready for him. Suddenly Gary was so busy, he didn't have time to worry about what people could or couldn't make him do.

"First off," Mrs. Block said, "I want you to know I've read every word any of your teachers ever wrote about you, and I've looked over all the testing you've had since you started school. Whew! What a job!" She pointed to a folder on her desk, crammed full of papers, with his name printed on the front of it in big red letters. "Also, as I'm sure you noticed, I spent all last week watching you."

"Why did you?"

"So I could find out about you for myself. To see if I agreed with the others."

"Did you?"

"Well, some of what other people said about you

seemed true to me. But a lot of what they said didn't."

"Didn't seem true?"

"Didn't seem true. Or didn't seem important. Or didn't seem to be the sort of thing I need to know about a student. I got a lot more information from watching you than I got out of reading what other people said.

"Do you want to know what I found out?" she asked. Gary wasn't sure. "None of it will really be news," she assured him.

"The most important thing I found out is that listening is by far your best learning tool. You understand what people say to you. You remember things you hear.

"About twenty percent of people—that's two people out of ten—are like you. We call you auditory learners," the teacher explained.

Gary frowned. "Is it bad?" he asked.

"It's not bad or good," said Mrs. Block.

"Will I outgrow it?" asked Gary.

"Why would you want to?"

"So I can be like everyone else."

"Nobody is like everyone else," said Mrs. Block. "Every egg is different."

She waited to make sure Gary was paying attention. Then she went on. "Here are some other things I saw last week: I saw that you're not comfortable in new spaces. That's called having trouble with spacial orientation. I saw that you're good at following directions if they're said out loud and if you understand them. I saw that you can work well alone if you know exactly what you're supposed to do and are given plenty of time to do it.

"I saw that you're friendly and curious about people but that you're afraid of them, too, which makes it hard for you to cooperate with them.

"I saw that you are worried and that being worried causes you to make mistakes.

"I saw that you're a good listener, that you're smart, and that you have much more potential than people said in these reports.

"I saw that your actual performance is much higher than your low test scores show. So I know that you don't test well, and I can't depend on tests to tell me about you."

"I always flunk," Gary said.

"And I saw that you're not a violent person," the teacher continued, "and that whatever happened between you and that boy on the playground—"

"Warren Firestone," Gary whispered.

"—is not going to happen again.

"I found out one thing from the reports that did interest me," Mrs. Block went on. "Your first-grade teacher said that you liked stories and that you could read the books she gave you."

"Not now."

"You can't read them now?"

"I can," Gary said. "But I don't like reading stories now. Or reading anything."

Mrs. Block thoughtfully tapped the eraser end of her pencil against her front teeth.

Gary felt uncomfortable. He hated to think about what he used to be able to do. He hated knowing that he had somehow lagged behind while the others had flown on ahead. He felt ashamed. Why hadn't he been able to keep up?

"You liked stories, and you could read some of them," Mrs. Block repeated.

"Those were baby books. They had big letters and little words," Gary explained.

"Yes," Mrs. Block said. Then, "I understand. And I know exactly what to try!"

Before Gary could say "I can't," he found himself holding several large books, a tape recorder, some cassettes, and a pair of oversized earphones that were so big, they looked like earmuffs.

The books were the same ones that other fourth- and fifth-graders were reading, Mrs. Block pointed out, except that these copies had extra-large print.

"How come?" asked Gary.

They were made for children who were partially blind, the teacher explained. The cassettes had been recorded for children who were completely blind, who needed to listen to the stories.

"I've found that using these large-print books and tapes together can be very helpful for auditory learners," Mrs. Block said.

"But I'm not blind!" protested Gary.

The teacher agreed. "That's true," she said. "Your eyesight is perfect. You don't even need glasses. But you are dyslexic, and that means reading is a hard skill for you to master. Your brain has to work super hard when you read. And if you're dealing with small print, your eyes have to work hard, too. After all, the smaller the print, the harder anyone's eyes have to work to read it.

"Using books with large print will make reading easier on your eyes. Then, even though reading will still be hard work for your brain, at least your eyes won't be tired and ready to give up before your brain is!"

"What about the tapes?" asked Gary.

"Auditory learners learn by . . ." Mrs. Block coached.

"Listening," Gary mumbled.

"If you hear the words at the same time you look at them, you'll make the connection between what you hear and what you see. And reading will get much easier," the teacher explained. "Especially after you get used to it."

"It sounds hard," Gary said.

"Everything sounds hard when someone tries to explain it," Mrs. Block said. "Think how hard it would sound if I tried to explain how to run or ride a bike—or eat with a knife and fork."

"I guess," Gary allowed.

"We'll be taking advantage of your strongest learning style and using your love of stories, too," said Mrs. Block.

"Who said I love stories?"

"You said you love stories. You said it to your first-grade teacher, and she wrote it down. I have the page she wrote on right here—somewhere."

Mrs. Block bent over to rummage about among

the papers, workbooks, books, reports, folders, notes, and scraps that covered the top of the table she called her desk.

Gary noticed that there was a white sock stuck to the back of her tan sweater. The sock and the sweater must have been in the clothes dryer together!

"Well, I can't find her report right now," the teacher said. "But I know it's what she said." With that, she waved Gary away and turned to other students, who were waiting.

Gary took all the stuff Mrs. Block had given him to his desk, which he had inched around so he could see out of the window. He liked to look out and be distracted.

For a while, he just sat there, staring out, not thinking, watching the fog fingers climb over the hill in back of the school.

When Mr. Cato came over to see how he was doing, Gary picked up the earmuff-sized headphones. "Why are these so big?" he asked the aide.

"So when you use them, you won't be able to hear anything except the words you're listening to. They'll block out all the other noises in the classroom that might distract you from your listening."

"What if there's a fire?" Gary asked. "How will I hear the bell?"

"If there's a fire, I'll come over and tap you on the shoulder," said Mr. Cato.

"What if Mrs. Block wants me and I don't hear her?" Gary asked.

Mr. Cato smiled. "If Mrs. Block wants you and you don't hear her, I'll come over and tip over your chair so you fall on the floor," he promised.

Gary looked at the aide. "That's silly," he said.

"But it will work," Mr. Cato said. "So you don't have any reason to worry about not hearing things. You can get on with your work and depend on me. I'll let you know if there's a fire or if Mrs. Block wants you."

"Or—" said Gary.

"Or anything," said Mr. Cato. "Now, let me show you how all these things work, so you can get started."

Mr. Cato helped Gary set up his machinery. Alec zipped past right before Gary put the huge earphones on. "Spaceman!" he sang out cheerfully, and he rapped Gary on the head with his sharp knuckles.

Nobody else paid any attention to Gary. Mrs. Block was busy with a thousand things, and her frazzly red head dipped and raised as she worked at her messy table with one student after another.

Gary took one of the books and looked at the title: *The Great Brain*. He opened it. The words were printed in large, clear type. He looked at the tape recorder. It was like his dad's. He knew how to work it. He found the tape that went with the book and put it into the machine. I'll do one page, he told himself, so nobody can say I didn't try.

Gary listened to the tape and read the words he was hearing. It was surprisingly easy.

By lunchtime, Gary had gotten so interested in the story that Mr. Cato had to touch his shoulder two times to let him know it was time to eat.

When Gary finally turned off the tape, closed the book, took off the earphones, and looked around, he saw Mrs. Block watching him. And for the first time since he'd come to her class, he saw what he thought might be a smile, or at least the beginning of one, on the teacher's face.

Remembering the sock stuck to the back of her tan sweater, Gary could not help smiling back.

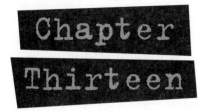

Chapter Thirteen

Gary liked taking the minibus back and forth to school. He felt safe. He knew the driver, Mr. Andrews, wouldn't let things get really out of hand. Once, when Jamahl and Alec were teasing one of the younger boys, Mr. Andrews pulled over and parked. He said he wasn't going to start again until they stopped. He would sit there just as long as he had to.

After they all were quiet, he said, "You kids remember, I got eyes in the back of my head. Nothing gets past me."

Alec made a face after Mr. Andrews got back into his seat, but the driver started up anyway. Then he said, "Eyes in the back of my head, Alec, just like I said. Watch yourself."

Everyone laughed.

Gary was always the last one picked up because he lived closest to school. Every day he waited on the front steps of his house and worried about whether Jesse would be on the bus.

If Jesse was there, he would be on the backseat, saving Gary a place. If Jesse wasn't there, Gary would sit with someone else. He would space out and try not to think about where Jesse was or why he had run away. He wondered whether Jesse would come back to Mrs. Block's class after they found him or maybe get sent to a different school, one for runaways, if there was such a place.

"Jesse says he doesn't know why he takes off," Gary told his mother. "He just gets this feeling, and he leaves. He says maybe he got it from his parents. They just took off one time and left him with his grandma and grandpa. They had itchy feet, his grandpa told him."

Gary's mother nodded. "Do you worry about him?" she asked.

"No," Gary fibbed. "I get mad at him. I think, what's he leaving for when he knows I like him to be at school with me?"

"I don't think Jesse's leaving has anything to do with you, Gary."

"I guess not," Gary said. "But if he liked me enough, maybe he'd stop running away. That would have something to do with me."

His mother thought. Then she said, "People don't change because someone else wants them to. They change because they want to, if they can."

"But we're friends," Gary objected. "We're best friends!" Gary had never been able to say that before about anyone. He loved the way it sounded. "We have fun together. Why does he have to go and mess things up?"

His mother couldn't answer. "It's nice you have a new friend, Gary," she said mildly.

"I have a bunch of new friends," he told her. "Everybody in this class is pretty much friends with everybody else."

"That's nice," his mother said.

"It's because we're all weirdos," Gary told her.

"Oh!" His mother sounded dismayed.

Gary didn't care. He didn't expect his mother to understand how good it felt to be in a class with a whole bunch of kids who could never satisfy Mr. Rudolph. Kids who could never in a million years make friends with Warren Firestone.

Warren Firestone. One morning, Gary looked

out the window of the bus and there he was, walking to school. In less time than it took to think "There's Warren," Gary's stomach curled into a knot and his mouth went dry.

Still, he couldn't stop looking. He even got up on his knees after the bus passed Warren and looked out the back window at him.

"What are you looking at?" Jesse wanted to know.

"Some kid I used to know," said Gary. Jesse looked out, too.

"Where?" he asked.

"Back there," answered Gary. "The one in the blue jacket."

Both boys watched as the bus moved on and the boy in the blue jacket appeared to grow smaller and smaller.

Finally, Gary turned and sat down again. "I can't see him anymore," he said. "He's way too small." Jesse sat down again, too. "He's nobody important, anyway," Gary told his friend. "We can just forget about him."

"Fine with me," Jesse said. "I already forgot."

"Me, too," said Gary.

The bus pulled into the small parking lot up

above Mrs. Block's school, and the children tumbled out. Marshall tried to say something to Gary that Gary didn't understand. Amanda had a hard time carrying her books and her puppy's traveling animal box, and Jesse helped her. Richard looked as if he might not make it through the door of the bus. And Jamahl blocked it on purpose and wouldn't let anyone behind him get out until Mr. Andrews made him move.

Then they all trailed down the hill, sort of together and sort of not, more or less ready to begin another day of school.

Chapter
Fourteen

Every day after lunch, Gary was supposed to work with Amanda and help her train the puppy. At first, Amanda didn't want to share her project with anyone. But Mrs. Block encouraged her to change her mind. "Sometimes two heads are better than one," the teacher said.

"Things haven't been very good in the puppy-training department lately," Amanda admitted to Gary, after she'd gotten to know him. "Maybe it will be better if there are two of us doing it."

The dog was a golden retriever named Shasta. "Guide dogs are almost always golden retrievers, Labrador retrievers, or German shepherds," Amanda told Gary. "Those are about the only breeds that can learn to do this kind of work. And even some of them can't." Amanda sighed. "Like maybe Shasta can't."

"What's she supposed to learn?" Gary asked.

"Nothing hard," Amanda grumbled. "Just 'simple obedience and social skills.' See?" She showed him her "Guide Dogs for the Blind" dog-training booklet and pointed to the part she'd just read.

"Are you Shasta's owner?" Gary asked, pulling the warm, wriggly puppy onto his lap and stroking the top of her smooth head.

"No," Amanda replied. "I'm the volunteer puppy-raiser. Some blind person will be her owner. Maybe."

"Maybe?"

"If she can learn what she's supposed to. Which I don't think she can."

"How old is this dog?" Gary wanted to know, taking the booklet from Amanda.

"She's eight months old already," Amanda said. "And I'm not even sure she always knows her own name yet." Amanda looked gloomily at the pup, now nestled in Gary's lap. "I think this dog might be learning disabled."

"Well," Gary said, "maybe she has special needs. She might need special teaching for her special needs. You know."

"Yeah, yeah," said Amanda impatiently. "But it's

a big drag to try to teach a dog with special needs."

"Exactly what's she supposed to learn?" he asked.

"Easy stuff," Amanda said. "First, she needs to recognize her own name and come when somebody calls her. After that, she has to learn to sit. And then stay. And then she has to learn to heel. Those are the basics. If she gets them, then she goes on to a real trainer to learn the hard stuff."

"How much time does she have to learn the basics?" Gary asked.

"She needs to know them by the time she's fifteen months old. And if she doesn't, she won't get to be trained to be a guide dog for the blind."

"What happens to her?"

"She just ends up as someone's pet," Amanda said.

"That's not so bad," Gary pointed out.

"Well, it's not like being a guide dog for someone who really needs you. And it's sort of like failing," said Amanda.

Gary wasn't sure he understood that. "Most dogs aren't guide dogs," he said. "They're not all failures."

"Most dogs don't have a chance to be guide dogs. If you have a chance and you blow it, that's failing," said Amanda stubbornly. "And it makes me a failure, too," she added.

Once he started working with the dog, Gary understood why Amanda felt so discouraged. He couldn't imagine Shasta learning all she needed to learn when she was having so much trouble recognizing her own name and coming when she was called.

One day, Gary and Amanda took the puppy outside. As she always did, she ran from one place to another, eagerly sniffing the ground.

"Shasta, come," Amanda called firmly. The puppy didn't even lift her head.

"Shasta, come!" Gary called sweetly. The puppy ignored him.

"If she obeys, we need to reward her," Amanda said.

"How?" asked Gary.

"Praise her. Say 'good dog' and pet her a lot. But so far, she hasn't gotten far enough to get much praise."

"She's really interested in smelling stuff," Gary observed.

"Their noses work better than their eyes do,"

Amanda explained. "Especially when they're little."

Gary thought about this. He sniffed his hands. They smelled from the detergent he'd washed with when he finished eating lunch. "Let me smell your hands, Amanda," he said.

"I will not!" Amanda put her hands behind her and took a step backward.

"Just let me smell them," Gary said. "I'm not going to hurt you."

Amanda hesitated and finally held out one hand, folded up. Gary sniffed it. Just as he thought. It smelled like detergent.

"I bet everything in the world smells better to this dog than we do," Gary decided. "And I bet if we smelled more like stuff she likes, we could teach her to come when we call her."

Gary and Amanda walked over to get the puppy. "What smell do you think would work?" Amanda asked.

Gary wasn't sure. He knew only one person who had trained dogs. And that was his father.

"My dad knows about dogs," he told Amanda as they took Shasta back to the school building. "I guess I could call and ask him."

"You could? When?" Amanda asked eagerly.

"I don't know," Gary hedged. "I'm not sure. I mean, he's really—um—busy. And he's mad at me, too."

Amanda didn't answer, but Gary could guess what she was thinking. "You think I shouldn't let that stop me," Gary said. "You think this is so important that I should call him, no matter how hard it is to talk to your father when he's mad at you." Amanda still didn't say anything. "Isn't that what you think?" Gary insisted.

"It would be hard," Amanda allowed. "But I think you should make yourself do it anyway. It might help a blind person. And Shasta. And us." Gary didn't answer. "But he's your father. You have to decide."

Gary said he would think it over.

Chapter
Fifteen

That night after dinner, Gary's mother sat down in her favorite old chair to watch TV and work on a needlepoint pillow she was making to give someone for Christmas.

Gary did two simple subtraction work sheets. That was the only homework he had. Restlessly, he wandered into the kitchen and looked in the refrigerator, but he wasn't hungry. Then he plopped down in front of the TV, but his mother was watching a show he didn't like. The telephone sat on the desk. Nobody called. The line was free. "I need to call Dad," he finally said.

"Go right ahead," his mother answered.

"I'm taking the phone into my room."

"Fine," she said.

"I need to ask him something about dogs," Gary explained.

"Gary," his mother said, "you have a right to talk to your father. You don't need to tell me what you're going to talk about."

Gary took the phone into his room and sat down with it on the floor by his bed. Three rings, then Goldy answered. As soon as Gary heard her voice, he hung up. He'd forgotten about Goldy.

He waited. Then he tried again. "Hello?" Goldy said. Gary hung up again.

He waited and waited. Then he tried one more time. This time his father's voice thundered over the line, "Who is this?" he roared. Gary choked. "Who is this? Better speak up!"

"Dad?" Gary said in a tiny voice. "It's me."

"Gary?" said his father. "You? I thought it was a crank caller. Somebody keeps ringing our number and then hanging up. I was going to tell them a thing or two."

"Oh," said Gary. "Well, it's just me."

Gary's father laughed. "Good thing I was mad at that crank caller," he said, "because I was planning to tell you a thing or two, too! Good timing, son." He laughed again.

Gary wasn't sure what to say, but at least his father seemed to be in a good mood.

"So what's doing, Gary? Are you ready for me to get you out of that joke of a school they put you in? I've been thinking this whole thing over. And I tell you, I don't think those people at your school know their elbows from their earlobes. I think you need different teachers. Like the ones at the Webster Academy. No nonsense over there about learning differences. Everybody learns the same, and everybody learns. Or else. What do you say, son? Doesn't that sound like the solution?"

"The Webster Academy?" said Gary.

"Uniforms and marching drills and everything," said his father. "All boys."

"Sounds—expensive," Gary said.

"Darn right. Your mother would have to pay her half, of course."

"Um, I don't know," Gary said. "I mean, I need to think about it."

"What's there to think about?"

"I—well, I just need to think about it, is all."

"I thought you'd jump at the chance, Gary." Gary didn't answer. "So what'd you call up for?" his father finally said.

"To ask you about dogs. For school."

"See? That's what I mean," the man said. "Dogs shouldn't have anything to do with school! Well, what about them?"

"Um, well, if you had a—a sort of dumb dog— and you wanted to teach it stuff, and it wouldn't learn, what would you do?"

"I'd whack it good until it learned to obey, and if that didn't do the trick, I'd take the worthless mutt to the pound and get a different dog."

"Oh," said Gary.

"That all?" his father asked.

"Uh-huh," said Gary. "Thanks."

"No problem," said his father. "And listen, I want you to think about my offer. Those people at the Webster Academy, they know how to handle a kid like you, believe me."

"I believe you," Gary said.

"Okay, then," said Mr. Harris. He hung up.

Webster Academy!

Gary put the telephone back. The TV was turned off now, and his mother was rolling up her needle-point.

"Dad wants me to change schools. He wants me to go to the Webster Academy," Gary told her.

His mother stood up. "That's nonsense," she said, more firmly than he'd ever in his life heard her say anything. "What's wrong with you staying where you are?"

"Dad says I'm in a joke of a school," Gary told her.

"It seems to me you're doing fine in your new school, Gary," his mother said. "I've talked to Mrs. Block on the phone, and I think she appreciates you better than any teacher you've ever had.

"The Webster Academy." She shook her head. "First, it's a bad idea. And second, it's very expensive."

"Dad said we could afford it if you pay half," Gary said.

"Well, I don't mean to pay half of anything I don't believe in," his mother answered.

"But Dad—" Gary began.

"Don't worry so much about your dad," his mother advised. "You should know by now that his bark is usually a lot worse than his bite."

That reminded Gary about what he'd called his father for in the first place.

"I didn't call him about schools, anyway," Gary

said. "I called him to see how to train a puppy to obey, if the puppy was hard to teach."

Gary's mother thought. "I knew a dog with a short attention span once," she said, "when I was a child. His master taught him with hot dogs."

"Hot dogs?"

"Yes," she recalled, "he would cut up a hot dog. Then he'd stand pretty close to the dog—at least at first—so the dog could smell it. He'd say, 'Here, Wilson'—that dog was named Wilson—and Wilson would smell the hot dog and come right over. And then he'd get a piece."

"That's a great idea, Mom!"

"The only trouble was, Wilson never learned to obey without the hot dogs. They had to bribe him to do it, even after he was a very old dog."

"Do you think that would happen with other dogs?" Gary asked.

"I've no idea," his mother answered. "I don't know a thing about dogs."

Gary found some hot dogs in the fridge. He cut one up and put the pieces into a Baggie to take with him to school in the morning. If he and Amanda could get Shasta to obey by bribing her, maybe later they could figure out a way to get her to do it without the bribe.

It's worth a try, he decided. Maybe after Shasta finds out we're going to praise her all over the place and pet her fur off if she learns, she'll think that's as good as getting a piece of a hot dog.

"She might," Mrs. Block agreed when Gary told her his plan the next day. Then the teacher tapped her front teeth with the eraser end of her pencil. "Hot dogs," she said thoughtfully. "Might work for kids, too." As usual, Gary wasn't sure whether Mrs. Block was joking or not.

After lunch, Gary and Amanda took Shasta outside. In no time flat, Shasta learned to come to them when they rewarded her with hot dog pieces.

Amanda took the credit. "Special teachers have special ways of teaching students with special needs," she bragged.

For the last half hour of school that day, they had a going-away party for Loretta. She was going back to her regular classroom. She had been in the county special ed class for three years, at first full-time, and then half-time. Now she was leaving.

At the party, they ate frosted cupcakes Mr. Cato had baked and drank fruit punch Ms. Sullivan brought. Then they all sat in a friendship circle to listen to Loretta's good-bye talk. It was the custom to give one, Gary found out, when you were leaving the special class.

Loretta stood up to give her talk, which she had written on a piece of paper. "When I first came here," she read, looking shy, "I was mad at everyone. I was mad at the teachers for not teaching me. I was mad at my family, too. I beat up on my sister. I was mad at myself. I scratched my face out of all the class pictures. I thought I was nothing.

"After I came here"—Loretta looked at Mrs. Block—"a *while* after I came here and worked hard, I found out I could learn. So I changed the way I was acting. And my whole life got better.

"The best part about this class was that I found out I could learn."

When she finished her talk, the children gathered around Loretta and high-fived her. Alec got excited and threw a piece of his cupcake across the room, and Shasta managed to scramble over the top of her pen and snag it.

Everyone was noisy except Mrs. Block. She sat quietly by herself, watching and not watching what was going on and looking satisfied—looking the way someone looks when they have a happy secret.

Chapter Sixteen

One Saturday afternoon, Jesse came over to Gary's house to play. Jesse's grandparents were worried that he might run away from Gary's, so they didn't bring his shoes.

"It's okay," Gary told Jesse after his grandparents had driven off. "We can play inside."

First, Jesse wanted to look through all of Gary's games and toys. He found a bucket of Legos and some pocket cars that Gary had forgotten he had. He found a Chinese checkers board, but no marbles. He found some Pick-Up-Stix, a Candy Land game, and a clown puppet. He found a big stack of construction paper.

"We can make paper airplanes and race them," Jesse decided.

Gary didn't know how to make paper airplanes. But Jesse showed him. Jesse folded the paper carefully to make sleek-looking planes that flew really well.

Gary's planes were lopsided and hardly flew at all.

"I don't like making things," he said, throwing his plane nose first onto the floor. "They're always wrong."

Jesse looked up from his plane. He was changing it in a way he thought would make it go farther. "You need to be patient when you're making something," he advised. "You need to concentrate."

"It's boring," Gary grumbled. "Let's do something else."

"Okay," said Jesse, "what?"

Gary had no idea what to suggest. "We could watch TV—or a video," he said.

"We don't have to be together to do that," Jesse reminded him.

"Well, we can't go outside," Gary said, as if that was why he was having trouble thinking of something to do.

"We can go out in your backyard," Jesse said. "I can play in the yard without my shoes."

The boys wandered outside. They sat down on the back steps.

"Now what?" Gary said.

Jesse shrugged.

There they sat.

This wasn't the way Gary had imagined it would be. He thought when Jesse came over, they'd just have fun.

"You're the guest," Gary said. "You get to decide."

"You're the host," Jesse said.

Gary's mother came out onto the porch. "I was just wondering," she said, "would you boys like to bake some cookies? We're all out, and I don't have time."

Both boys brightened. Baking cookies sounded like a perfect thing to do.

Mrs. Harris tied big aprons around each of the boys. She set out everything they needed for cookie baking, and then she went about her business.

The boys both had baked cookies before, and they knew how to do it. They measured and mixed and soon had a big bowl of cookie batter. Then they put in the chocolate chips.

It was time to heat the oven, put the batter on cookie sheets, and bake.

"I like batter even better than I like cookies," Jesse said, licking his fingers.

"So do I!" Gary agreed.

The boys looked at each other.

Gary got two cereal bowls and two spoons. He held his finger to his lips. Then he spooned half the batter into one bowl and half into the other.

He and Jesse tiptoed out onto the back porch. They were careful to close the door quietly behind them.

They sat close together on the steps, giggling and eating cookie batter. Everything seemed funny.

"When I get washed up for dinner," Jesse told Gary, "my grandma always says, 'Give those hands more than a lick and a promise!'" He licked some batter off his fingers.

"A lick and a promise," chuckled Gary.

"And you know what?" Jesse said. "Sometimes, instead of brushing my teeth, I just wet the tooth-brush and put it back in the glass."

"Me, too," said Gary.

They sat quietly for a few minutes, scraping the last bit of batter out of their bowls. Then Jesse said, "Want to play Ha-Ha-Ha?"

"Ha!" said Gary, beginning the game.

"Ha-ha!" said Jesse, with a very serious face.

"Ha-ha-ha!" countered Gary, with an even more serious face.

"Ha-ha-ha-ha!" Jesse almost smiled but didn't.

"Ha-ha-ha-ha-ha!" Gary almost laughed but didn't.

"Ha-ha-ha-ha-ha-ha!" It was the best Jesse could do. He looked at Gary's super-serious expression and at the batter on his nose and broke into a real laugh. Gary had been having trouble keeping a straight face. As soon as Jesse laughed, Gary laughed, too.

"Ha-ha-ha-ha-ha-ha-ha!" both boys laughed, pointing at each other and then laughing all the harder.

After a while, they went back inside. Gary's mother had cleaned up the kitchen. They put their bowls and spoons in the sink and rinsed off their sticky hands. Then they went into Gary's room and played Go Fish! until Jesse's grandparents came to pick him up.

The next week at school, Jesse took off again. Then he came back. Gary sat next to him on the morning bus. "Why'd you run away this time?" he demanded. Jesse made a face. "Where'd you go?" Jesse breathed on the window and wrote *J* on the fogged-up part. "Are you going to do it again?" Jesse shrugged.

When they got to school and all burst noisily into the classroom, Mrs. Block was at her table, already working. The teacher stood up to greet her students.

Gary saw that one of Mrs. Block's stockings was twisted around her leg and that her sweater was buttoned wrong. He wondered how the teacher would act if he told her.

"You buttoned your sweater wrong, Mrs. Block," he could say. Would she look down and be surprised and self-conscious and button it over again, quickly, so she wouldn't have to feel embarrassed? That's what he did when someone told him he'd been careless and buttoned wrong. Or would she just frown at him?

"Mrs. Block, Mrs. Block!" Everyone wanted the teacher's attention.

"Good morning, good morning," she said as she handed out papers and workbooks and books and cassettes and pens and pencils and board games and puzzles. She told this one to go to the computer and that one to work in the other room where it was quiet and a third to put on his glasses if he hoped to get anything accomplished and a fourth to wash her face and try to wake up, please.

To Jesse she said, "Hand them over!" Jesse sat down on the floor, pulled off his shoes, and gave them to her.

Finally, Gary was the only one waiting. Mrs. Block was already hunched over a stack of materials, muttering to herself. She was searching for something and soon became so frustrated that she started tossing papers back over her shoulder and onto the floor behind her.

Gary felt alarmed. He had never seen a grown person do such a thing. "Your sweater's wrong!" he cried out nervously.

The teacher immediately stopped her search, took off her glasses, and whirled her chair around so she was facing Gary. "Wrong?" she inquired. "And what, may I ask, is wrong with it?"

Gary wished he hadn't spoken. "I just meant you've got the buttons stuck into the wrong button-holes," he said miserably.

"And who says that's wrong?" the teacher asked.

"I do, I guess," he mumbled.

Now Mrs. Block looked at her sweater.

"Never mind, Mrs. Block," Gary said. "It doesn't matter."

"It might," she said.

"Oh, I don't think it does. I mean, it's buttoned," he said.

"Then why did you bother to tell me it was wrong?" Mrs. Block persisted.

"Well, when I don't button right, people tell me it's wrong. They tell me to do it over." He looked away from the teacher. "They make fun of me."

"Did you want to make fun of me?"

"No," Gary stammered. "I just wanted to . . ." He couldn't finish.

"Criticize me?" she asked. "Help me?" she suggested. Gary's ears burned. He knew they were bright red.

"The fact is, my sweater *is* buttoned wrong. I was in a rush getting ready this morning. And I didn't get the right buttons into the right holes." She undid her sweater and buttoned it up again.

"Thanks for pointing out my mistake," she continued. "It was kind of you to tell me before someone criticized me or made fun of me. I appreciate your help."

Just then, the telephone, which was perched half on and half off the top of a tall, battered filing cabinet, began to ring.

"You get that, Gary," Mrs. Block said, raising her voice so he could hear her over the loud ring. "Say 'County special ed, Gary Harris speaking. How can I help you?'"

Gary picked up the phone. "County special ed," he said timidly. On the other end, he heard the explosion of a familiar loud and impatient voice.

"What?" the voice demanded. "Ed who?"

"It's my father!" Gary cried, tossing the telephone like a hot potato to Jesse, who was passing by on his way to the pencil sharpener.

Jesse took over and recited what they were all taught to say when they answered the phone at school. "County special ed, Jesse Green speaking. How can I help you?"

Gary could hear his father's voice, but he couldn't make out what he was saying. Jesse held the receiver away from his ear and made a face. Mrs. Block looked curious. The puppy yipped and jumped against the side of her pen.

"Hello? Hello?" called Mr. Harris's voice, loud, yet small and distant, too, coming out of the telephone.

Jesse giggled. Gary waited tensely. Mrs. Block pushed herself away from her table and rolled her chair over so she could take the phone from Jesse. She waved the boys away.

When she finished speaking to Mr. Harris, the teacher stood to put the telephone back onto the top of the tall file. Then she sat down again and rolled herself back to her table. She frowned and fiddled with the buttons on her saggy sweater.

"My father thinks reading doesn't matter," Gary said.

"So he just told me," the teacher replied.

"My father says he knows how to read perfectly well and that he never does it anyway. He says that with videos and tapes and TV and all, nobody needs to worry about reading anymore. He says he hasn't read in years and that it doesn't make one bit of difference."

Mrs. Block leaned back in her chair, frowning thoughtfully. "He could be right," she said.

"He could?"

"There are plenty of people who seem to get by without reading much of anything. Personally, I don't care whether people read or not," said the teacher.

"You don't?" Gary was amazed.

"Nope, I don't care whether people read or not," Mrs. Block went on, fixing her pale eyes on him. "But I jolly well care whether they *can* read. I care whether they're able to. I care whether they have the choice. I think everyone deserves to have the choice.

"If people choose not to read, that will have to

be okay with me. But if they can't read and don't have a choice, that's not okay.

"It's the choice I care about. And if people can't read in the first place, they can't choose not to, can they?"

"I guess not," Gary said hesitantly.

"Right!" said the teacher, sounding satisfied. "I'm glad you and I got that straightened out!"

Chapter Eighteen

Gary had been in Mrs. Block's class for four months. Thanksgiving and Christmas, Valentine's Day and Presidents' holiday all had come and gone. But just when he'd quit worrying about it, Mrs. Block told Gary it was time for her to have a meeting with him and his parents. She gave him a note to give to his mother. "What should we do with the one for your father?" she asked.

"I guess I could give it to him. If I see him."

Mrs. Block raised her eyebrow. "What about the mail?" she suggested.

She got out an envelope and a stamp. "Do you want to read the note before I send it?" she asked.

Gary could see that this note was typed. It was short. The words looked easy. He took it from Mrs. Block.

The note said,

```
To the parents of Gary Harris:

Your son is doing well in my class.
I would like to meet you both and
talk with you about plans for Gary's
curriculum for the rest of this
school year.

                    Yours truly,
                    Mrs. Maribeth Block,
                    Teacher
```

"*Cur-ric-u-lum?*" Gary asked.

"What you're going to work on," Mrs. Block answered. "Think they'll come?"

"They have to come, don't they?" Gary asked.

"Well, they're supposed to," Mrs. Block said, "but some parents don't. You'd be surprised. Some of them just call up and complain. And some don't even do that."

"They'll come," he said with a sigh. "They always do."

"I want you to be at the meeting, Gary," Mrs. Block said. "We're not going to say anything you can't hear."

Gary remembered the last meeting he'd gone to

with his parents and his teachers. "I don't like those meetings," Gary said.

"This will not be one of 'those' meetings," the teacher promised.

Still, Gary didn't want to be there. He didn't want to hear his father shout. And he didn't want to see his mother look sad.

But more than that, he didn't want either of his parents to see anything they wouldn't like: not the messy rooms, not the odd teacher, not the unusual students. He didn't want his mother and father to find out that he was a weirdo, that they were all weirdos here. He was afraid his parents wouldn't understand.

"I don't want them to come here!" he cried.

"And why not, may I ask?" said the teacher. How could he explain without hurting her feelings?

"Because—I don't think they're going to like it. And I don't think they're going to let me stay."

Mrs. Block looked serious. "I think it will be good for both of us to find out what they think," she said. "So be sure to mail the letter to your father. And don't forget to give your mother the note. I'll be expecting to hear from both of them."

The meeting was arranged swiftly, for the following Monday right after school. And, at 2:30 precisely, to Gary's horror, his father appeared, walking toward the school at exactly the moment the noisy children passed in the other direction, headed for the minibus.

Jesse, carrying his shoes on top of a mountain of papers and books, could barely see where he was going and almost smacked right into Mr. Harris.

The man stood perfectly still and watched with a frown on his face while the children straggled past. Then he brushed off his sleeves with his hands, straightened his already perfectly straight clothing, and strode toward the school.

Gary watched from the shadow of the building, feeling his stomach turn into what felt like a knot, pulled tight. Then he ducked back inside. "My father's here!" he called.

Mrs. Block hurried out of the restroom. She had brushed her hair, but the bristly red curls were already popping out of place. She had put on lipstick, and the pink color on her lips made her white face look even paler than usual. She had put on a different sweater, too, a blue one with white beads stitched around the neck. Gary could tell this had once been a fancy sweater, but now it looked just about as tired as the tan one she usually wore. And it was buttoned wrong.

"So," she said, "time for Mater and Pater. Chin up! Shoulders back!"

"Mater and Pater?" said Gary.

"Latin for Mother and Father," Mrs. Block explained. Then she gathered together Gary's books and workbooks and papers and cassettes and set them down on one of the long, low tables where students worked when they weren't at their desks. She swiped at the table with her sleeve, to make sure it was clean, and then she got four chairs and grouped them at one end.

From the doorway, Mr. Harris cleared his throat. Mrs. Block and Gary looked up. There stood Gary's father, dressed in a white warm-up suit with shiny silver trim. His silver-gray hair gleamed. And his white athletic shoes looked brand new.

"You must be Gary's dad," said Mrs. Block. "Please come in and have a seat."

Mr. Harris walked slowly across the room toward the table. His eyes took in everything.

Mrs. Block stood up very straight and nervously cleared her throat. She put out her hand. "How do you do, Mr. Harris," she said, "I'm Gary's teacher, Mrs. Block." She followed the man's gaze around the room. "We have a busy classroom, as you can see," she said. "With every child here working individually, that is, on his or her own level, at his or her own pace, housekeeping has to take a backseat."

"Where's the classroom?" Gary's father asked.

"This is the main classroom," said Mrs. Block.

"I've never seen a classroom like this before," Mr. Harris argued. "Where are the rows of desks and the chalkboards? Where's the front? Where's the back?"

"We don't put our desks in rows here," Mrs. Block explained. "In our classrooms, students move from one workstation to another. And students spend a lot of time working alone, at their own speed. We don't have a front or a back. It's not the way we need things to be set up."

Gary could see that his father was as angry with Mrs. Block as he had been with Mr. Rudolph. In public, his father was angry at the teachers. In private, he was angry at Gary.

In spite of Mrs. Block's promise, Gary now felt sure that this parent–teacher conference would be just like all the other ones. Maybe even worse. He knew he didn't want to be there. He urgently needed to escape.

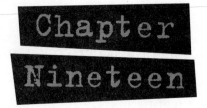
Practice makes perfect. Gary could escape anytime he wanted. This time, he let go of his mind quickly, the way you let go of the string of a helium balloon. And he watched it take off into the clear sky, a red balloon growing smaller and smaller as it gained altitude and sped away.

Gary's face was turned toward the window. His eyes looked empty. His mouth hung slightly open. His mind was vacant.

As if it reached his ears from a great distance, Gary heard his mother's voice. "Knock-knock," she said softly from the doorway.

"Come on in, Mrs. Harris," said Mrs. Block. "We were waiting for you."

Gary's mother and father nodded "hello" to one another, and Mrs. Block shook hands with Mrs. Harris. Then they sat down in the too-small chairs. Gary sat, too. Gary's father frowned at the little chair. Then he turned it around and straddled it, resting his arms on the back.

"I thought it was time for the four of us to get together," Mrs. Block said. "Gary's had a chance to adjust to us, and I've had time to get to know Gary. But before I begin, let me try to answer any questions you might have."

The balloon that was Gary's attention was now only a tiny spot far up in the sky, so far away that it didn't even have a color. Gary could hear everything Mrs. Block and his parents were saying, but none of it mattered. Because he was not really present. He was not really there with them. He was just a tiny speck up in the sky, sailing off by himself to some other and much more comfortable place.

"When's Gary going back to a real classroom with regular kids?" Gary's father asked. He was on the attack.

"I'm not sure," Mrs. Block replied calmly. "But I'd guess it won't be for several years."

"Years!" Mr. Harris exploded.

Mrs. Block continued. "Since Gary came to this class," she said, "his work has been remarkable."

"Remarkably good or remarkably bad?" barked Mr. Harris.

"That's a fair question," said the teacher. "You're reminding me to be more specific. I'll begin again. Since he came to my class, Gary has done very good work."

Both of Gary's parents looked interested. The balloon stopped its headlong flight. It seemed to hesitate.

"Gary has made friends," Mrs. Block went on. "He takes part in all of our activities. He's usually kind to others, helpful, cooperative, and socially appropriate. I feel optimistic about his future." The balloon of Gary's attention now began to drift slowly down.

"Extremely optimistic," the teacher repeated.

The balloon was falling faster now. Gary could see its bright red color. He could see the string attached to it moving back and forth underneath, like a friendly arm waving hello.

No teacher had ever said a single good thing about Gary before. He sneaked a glance at his parents. His mother looked surprised and interested. But his father looked doubtful and sly, as if he would soon get to the bottom of this.

"You don't find Gary slow?" asked Mr. Harris.

"Oh, yes," Mrs. Block said. "I do. Gary works very slowly. His slow rate of working is one of the learning disabilities Gary has to live with."

"How will he keep up?" Mr. Harris demanded to know.

The balloon quivered, but stayed put.

"Keep up?" Gary heard the teacher ask.

"With the others?"

"He can't. That's one reason he's here. The way we work, everyone goes at his or her own pace, learning as quickly and as well as he or she can. Nobody needs to keep up with anyone else."

Gary's mother broke in, "Do you find Gary distractible?" she asked. "Teachers have always complained about that."

"Yes," said Mrs. Block, "Gary is highly distractible. That's why we turned his desk around to face the wall."

"Well, that's just dandy, Mrs. Stone," said Gary's father.

"Block," she corrected him, "Mrs. Block."

For a moment, Mr. Harris seemed flustered. Then he continued. "That's just fine in a schoolroom, Mrs. Block. But what about out in the real world? How is Gary supposed to manage out there? Is his boss going to turn Gary's desk around when he finds out he's distractible?"

Ha! I've got you there! the look on Mr. Harris's face plainly said.

The balloon started drifting away again. Gary stared blankly at nothing. He could hear the grown-ups' voices, but he let the words run into one another, and they quickly became sounds without meanings.

"The real world," Mrs. Block began to answer Mr. Harris's question. But before she could finish, Gary's mother spoke up.

"What's not real about this world?" Mrs. Harris asked in a challenging way, gesturing at the room around them. Her voice was so full of energy that the balloon behaved as if someone had grasped the string and given it a good, hard tug.

Before Gary could begin to even try to understand what was happening, he felt the red balloon quickly descending, making a beeline back to Mrs. Block's classroom.

"And what's so much more real about your world, I'd like to know?" Gary's mother was addressing his father. "A world full of stairs and rowboats and bikes and skis and treadmills that never stop moving and never go anywhere?"

Gary's mother was talking about the exercise machines at his father's health and fitness club. Mr. Harris frowned, but he didn't answer.

Gary could not tell what it was that stumped his father and kept him from arguing. Was it his mother's question, or was it the new, energetic way she asked it?

When the balloon got close enough, Gary grabbed hold of the string and wound it around his finger. He didn't want his attention sailing off again. He wanted to listen to every single thing that was being said.

"That's the point, isn't it?" Mrs. Block put in. "This world is the real world for Gary right now. It's the world he works well in, and it's the world he needs to be in. What world he will need next, nobody knows."

"And it doesn't matter, either," said Gary's mother. "What matters is what's happening right now. Gary's learning. And he's not so angry or lonely or discouraged anymore. He has friends.

Whatever world he's in, it's his size. It fits him. He's comfortable in it. That's all that matters, so far as I'm concerned."

Gary saw different expressions pass one after another across his father's face. His father looked surprised. Then he looked confused. And then he looked relieved.

Mr. Harris turned to the teacher. "So," he said in a take-charge voice, as if he were the one who was running this meeting, "you feel my son's doing all right here in your class, do you?"

Matter-of-factly, Mrs. Block opened her grade book and turned it so Mr. Harris could see the grades. "As and Bs," she pointed out. "Some gold stars. And all assignments completed. I call that okay, don't you?"

"Well," said Mr. Harris, "I certainly do. Yes. Nothing wrong with grades like that, no matter what class someone's in. Isn't that right?" He looked at Gary's mother.

"Yes," she agreed, "that's right. There's nothing wrong with grades like that."

◼ ◼ ◼

After the meeting, Gary and his parents left the building together and went out into the twilight. A new moon—a sliver of pale light—was shining in the navy blue sky.

When they reached the parking lot, Gary's mother said, "It was nice to see you, Horace. Give my regards to Goldy." She rested her hand on Gary's shoulder. Gary was surprised to find that he liked the way his mother's hand felt there. It was soft, but not too soft.

"Well, yes, nice to see you, Elizabeth," Gary's father said, "and you, too, son. Keep up the good work." He reached out and rested his hand on Gary's other shoulder. Gary was surprised to find that he liked the way his father's hand felt, too. It was hard, but not too hard.

Something was different. . . . Something had changed. And whatever it was, Gary was sure Mrs. Block had made it happen. But he knew that if he asked her about it, she would say she had no idea what he was talking about and that he'd better get down to work, pronto, or she would make herself a note to remind his parents about the Webster Academy next time she saw them.

Chapter Twenty

It was Mrs. Harris's night to have dinner out at a restaurant with her friend Mavis. Gary decided to cook himself a burrito for his supper.

First he browned the meat in a frying pan and splattered grease all over the top of the stove. Then he heated refried beans in a pot and carelessly let some of the beans stick to the bottom. When he opened the package of flour tortillas, crumbs fell onto the floor. When he grated the cheese, cheese bits sprayed all over the place. And when he chopped the lettuce, pieces of lettuce flew this way and that.

The kitchen, right then, could have been declared a federal disaster area. But Gary wasn't through.

Next he sat down at the table and ate. When he finished, he left his dirty plate and his greasy, crumpled paper napkin and the sticky bottle of hot sauce on the table. He got milk out of the refrigerator, poured some into a glass, and spilled some onto the counter. He drank the milk, left the glass in the sink, the milk carton on the counter, and the spilled milk dripping down into the silverware drawer, which he hadn't bothered to close.

Just as he was about to turn out the light and leave the kitchen, his mother poked her head in to say good-bye.

"I'm going now, Gary," she said.

"Bye, Mom."

"The telephone number of the restaurant is right by the phone, in case you need me."

"Okay."

"I won't be late."

"Okay."

Gary started to walk out of the kitchen, but his mother stopped him. "By the way," she said, with a hint of that special new energy behind her soft voice, "now that Mrs. Block has told me how capable you are"—she paused—"I expect to find a spotless kitchen waiting for me when I get home!"

"What?" cried Gary. "You what?"

"Good-night, Gary," his mother called, closing the front door behind her.

A spotless kitchen! Gary's mother had never expected him to clean up after himself. He'd always left his messes for her to take care of.

He looked around. Grease spattered the stove. Hot sauce splotched the table. Cheese bits stuck to the walls. Dishes, glasses, and silverware needed washing. The pot and pan he'd used needed scrubbing. The floor needed sweeping. The counters and the table needed wiping. Why, it would take him all night to clean up the mess he'd made in the kitchen. All night!

"All night? Then you'd better get cracking," said a familiar voice. That voice—he knew it was inside his own head. But it was her voice, anyway. Mrs. Block's.

He got out a sponge and started on the stove.

Chapter
Twenty-one

One lunchtime in the spring, Gary and Jesse ate outside, sitting on a big tree stump at the top of the path. "Moonball is a baby game," Gary said, unwrapping his egg-salad sandwich.

"Yuk!" said Jesse, "egg salad stinks."

"I get tired of peanut butter," Gary said.

"I don't," said Jesse.

"Moonball is a baby game," Gary repeated.

"So what?" asked Jesse. "It's fun. And it's easy. Anybody can play. Even you!"

"Take that back," Gary said.

"Take what back?" asked Jesse.

"Take back that I'm a bad athlete!"

"Okay," said Jesse, "I take it back. You're not a bad athlete. You're a terrible athlete! You can hardly even play moonball, that's what a terrible athlete you are."

When the boys got through wrestling around in the weeds, they climbed back up on the stump and ate.

"Are you planning to run away again soon?" Gary asked.

Jesse shrugged. "You know I don't plan to do it. It just happens."

"You don't have to let it," Gary reminded his friend.

"I know," the boy said. "But I might let it. So it's better for Mrs. Block to keep my shoes."

"Mrs. Block can't keep your shoes for you for the rest of your life."

"I'm not talking about the rest of my life," Jesse said. "I'm talking about now. Anyway, what difference does it make to you?"

Now it was Gary who shrugged. He pushed the straw into his juice container. "I was just hoping you wouldn't do it anymore," he said.

"Do you worry about me?" Jesse wanted to know.

"Sort of," Gary allowed.

"Do you miss me?"

"Yes," Gary admitted. "Anyway, when you run away, where do you run to?"

"One time I went to the bus station," Jesse said.

"Where else?" Gary asked.

"To a movie."

"Was it fun?" Gary asked.

"No," Jesse said. "It was scary. When I run away, everything is scary."

"Then why would you want to do it again?"

"I don't want to do it again. I'm afraid I'll do it again."

"You're really weird, Jesse, you know?" said Gary.

Jesse rolled up the paper bag from his lunch. He jumped off the stump. "Weird!" he cried. "Look who's talking!" He threw the bag at Gary and took off toward the field, where some of the other kids were playing Statue.

Gary followed, and when he almost caught up, he threw the bag back at Jesse. "Missed by a mile, spaceman!" cried Jesse.

"Next time, weirdo!" called Gary.

"Get out of the way if you're not in the game," shouted Alec.

Gary and Jesse joined the others and played

Statue until the lunch recess was over. Then the two boys walked back to class with their arms around each other's shoulders.

"Be careful not to step on my feet," Jesse warned.

Gary was careful.